Street Wealthy

Season One

LARRY DARDEN

Fulton Books, Inc.
Meadville, PA

Published by Fulton Books 2020

ISBN 978-1-64654-682-4 (Paperback)
ISBN 978-1-64654-683-1 (Digital)

Printed in the United States of America

The Pilot

E verything in life happens for a reason. The people you meet and the places you go, it all helps create your story. Speaking of stories, let me tell you about J.R Jones. He was a typical kid, but his upbringing was rough and his family struggled. He had a little sister that he felt that he had to protect her whole life. Nevertheless, bad times and good times, good choices and bad choices all formed his circumstances, making him who he was and determined his destiny. He grew up in the heart of Suffolk, Virginia—the largest city in the state land wise but not in population. His father detailed cars for a dealership called Mike Duman, and his mother was a housewife who kept him and his sister clean, fed, and who taught them every fundamental thing she learned in life. His little sister's name was Karissa, and there was a ten-year age difference between them. But they were really close and had a tight bond. He started his childhood growing up on the east side of town in Heritage Acres Apartments and then moved to Freeney Avenue. His father was a heavy drinker and loved partying with his friends. He dealt with a lot of other women behind J.R's mother's back. I guess he wasn't happy with where he was in his life. He got married young and had J.R in his early twenties. He was just living life and stayed lit until it landed him in rehab. J.R constantly saw his father in this manner and decided he would be nothing like that.

Now when J.R got older, as the old heads would say, he hopped off the porch early. He started moving through the streets a li'l bit and moved across town to the west side of downtown on Pine Street, which ran into Mahan and Church Street. This area was much more violent and heavier with drugs than where he started out as a kid. Even though the east side wasn't a walk in the park either, it was just that the west side was a little faster; and being in that fast environment, he caught an interest in it and wanted to make money. He got tired of seeing his parents' struggle. He got out there and started learning the game and came up a li'l bit, fell off, came up again, and made mistake after mistake; but he learned from them. He met an older guy named Steph who was a big boy in the hood, the biggest drug dealer J.R had ever seen. Steph was moving heroin, cocaine, and weed in big weight. J.R had never seen so many drugs in one place or so many corner boys having to go through one person. Steph would pull up in Cadillacs, Range Rovers, Audis, Benzes, and BMWs with super bad chicks that were dressed really nice. Their hair was nice and they smelled really good, with perfect makeup. They were always smiling and happy. J.R knew immediately that he wanted to be like Steph and tried to get down with his team several times, but Steph always denied him, saying that he wanted him to get his education, play sports or do music. Everybody in the hood knew J.R could rap his ass off and loved music, but rapping wasn't putting no money in his pockets at that point. So he stayed persistent and finally wore Steph down to take him under his wing so he could level up and start making real money. Steph set him up in a good position. By the time he was nineteen, J.R had his own place and was able to help his parents and do more for his little sister.

The Beginning

Over the years, Steph had gotten way too big, and the feds ran in on him. And with the feds having a 98 percent conviction rate, it was almost impossible for Steph to get out of the situation, even with the best lawyers his money could buy. Not having any evidence of Steph touching or moving anything, they only convicted him on conspiracy charges through informants snitching to save their own asses, putting him away for twelve years. When he was released, a lot of the guys he left behind on the streets that were hustling for him—well, at least, the ones that were still on the street, in the game, and not locked up—paid their debt. They hit Steph with any money they owed him, which was about three or four hundred thousand. He took that money and began an independent record label.

Steph found a lot of talent and put money behind a lot of artists. One rapper he took particular interest in was a guy named Ron Ron. His real name was DuRon from Virginia Beach, the Bridle Creek neighborhood. Steph took him under his wing. He also thought back to the old days and remembered how good of a rapper J.R was, but he knew by now that J.R had probably already passed all that. And Steph wasn't sure that he could convince him to get out of the streets and sign to his label. He went to J.R and had a sit-down with him, "Look, I know how it is, and I know what you're doing. I put you in the game, but I want you to get out before shit hits the fan. I don't want you to turn out like me. I don't want you to see the inside of a cell, ever. You don't want to witness that part of the game. Quit while you can and are ahead. Take this chance with me and my record label. Have I ever steered you wrong?"

It took about three or four months to convince J.R to leave the streets, but he finally did. The first thing Steph did was work with Ron Ron, hitting him with a five-thousand-dollar budget to do his project. That five racks covered studio time, features, beats, and all that goes with it. J.R helped out and made a lot happen with the connections he made while he was in the streets, with good producers and quality studios. They went a little over budget, but J.R covered it. He was fresh out of the street, and his pockets were still heavy. Ron Ron ended up making a dope-ass album, and it sold digitally and physically. It made them more money than Steph had to begin the label with. They decided to put out a volume 2 using the same producers that he had from the first one. Major labels saw him come up, and Steph's phone started ringing off the hook. Things were looking way up at this point. After having meetings after meeting with several majors, they went with the best deal for a partnership. One of the majors even talked Steph into using different producers and high-dollar features for volume 2, but J.R wasn't with it and tried to talk him out of it. Long story short, the album was way left field from the original. It was too commercial, and it didn't create the same buzz, causing them to lose a lot of money because the budget was bigger than the sales recoup. If Steph would have listened to J.R, stayed 100 percent independent, and used the same budget and producers, they would have made money and continued to come up.

The major label panicked. They threatened to sue Steph and pressured him to get rid of Ron Ron, and eventually he did. J.R didn't like that. He didn't want to see Ron Ron struggle and was going to try to help him, but Steph told J.R to leave Ron Ron alone and that he was no longer his business. J.R fought and fought for Ron Ron because at this point, he felt like they were family. Steph just couldn't understand why J.R was so adamant about Ron Ron staying. J.R finally manned up and told Steph, "If Ron Ron goes, I go too." That is exactly what J.R did. He left and told Ron Ron, "We are going to create another project using the formula from the last album. We don't have a record label, but I have a few dollars left from the streets and I am going to invest it into you. I'm going to get you another deal." J.R went to a lot of different major labels and found out that the label that worked with Steph was blackballing Ron Ron. J.R started thinking about how they would pull this off.

Cruising through the city one afternoon, J.R was listening to Ron Ron's first project while going down East Washington Street. He had a full tank, but as he rolled up on this gas station, there was this beautiful female pumping her own gas. She was about five feet and five inches, and she had a caramel complexion. She had her hair in a ponytail and was thick and curvy in all the right places. He pulled into the gas station and parked next to her pump. "Excuse me, how are you doing today?"

She responded, "I'm good. You?"

J.R said, "I'm good. I wish I would have gotten here earlier. I could have helped you with that."

"With which, pump it or pay for it?"

"Both."

"Really now? What comes with that?"

"Well how about telling me your name first?"

"Why do you need to know my name? It's not like you're going to give me my gas money back."

"Ummm, al...most...there. Yeah, now, I'm done."

"Okay. What did you spend?"

"Thirty-six dollars and eighty-nine cents."

"Okay, well here is forty dollars. Now I need your name."

"Mmmmm, so you just go around handing out money to cute girls, huh?"

"Well, no. I give money to attractive women, and I would like to know your name."

"Thank you for the compliment. My name is Tianna."

"Hello, Tianna. I would like to get to know you better."

"Is that short for you need a booty call for paying for my gas? Because if that is so, you can take this forty—"

"Yo, shorty, I mean Tianna, chill. I just want to get to know you. I don't want anything in return for the forty dollars."

"Oh, okay. Well, give me your phone, and I will put my number in it."

"If I give you my phone, you will have to call yourself so I know I don't have a bogus number. Tell me now if you don't want to talk so I don't waste my time. Do you have a man?"

"Nah, I got a friend, but it ain't serious. Besides, you seem like a legit guy."

She put the number in his phone and called herself. Then she said, "Thank you." And she sped away like she was late for an appointment. Whatever fragrance she was wearing lingered in the air and intoxicated his senses until his phone rang and caught him off guard. When he looked at it, he saw that it was Deja calling. She was fam from the east side. Even though he moved away, they were still close. See, when J.R was hustling, he used Deja's house as his stash place. In return, he paid her bills. Deja also had a daughter, who was now three. Since he was in a position to help, he helped her with whatever she needed.

"Yo, Dej, what's up?"

"I need to talk to you about something serious."

"Not on the phone. You know that."

"Okay, I know. I know. But I really need you."

"Aiight, Dej. I'm on my way."

So he was rolling to Deja's house, still thinking about Tianna and listening to Ron Ron. He pulled up to Deja's house, and her little girl ran out to meet him. Deja was close behind her. They both gave him hugs. "What's up, Deja?"

"Well, J.R, when you were hustling, I was in a great position, and I never had to worry about anything. But now, even though you took care of me when you had the record deal, my pockets are almost flat. I guess I was trying to live the high life that you got me used to and—"

"Look, Dej, I didn't get you used to anything. It was fast money, and you used it as such because you always thought that it would be rolling in. I told you that I would not always be in the game, and I guess you didn't believe me."

"J.R, it's not that. I got a few people I trust, and if you get me plugged in to your old connect, then I can run and flip myself. I just want it like I had it. This nine-to-five job got me living a little over paycheck to paycheck. I want to be a little more than comfortable. You feel me?"

"Dej, when I was in the business, there were a lot of bumps and bruises that I had to take the fall for, and I can't let you do that because of your baby girl. I don't have any attachments. I also can't let you do that because you don't have any pull or power in the streets."

"But J.R, I can do it. I can get pull or power. If I need to, she can go stay with my mom, and I can focus on hustling 24-7."

"No, Dej, it doesn't work like that. You mess up, and they find your loved ones, sweetie. Look, if you need me to flip a few bricks so you can get a stack, I will. You will need to stay on the straight and narrow for baby girl."

Deja was upset, saying, "Oh, so now you're the law on being straight. All those years you were using my house to stash shit."

"Dej, I also paid your bills, and I ain't get no pussy or even a home-cooked meal." They both laughed. "Don't start with me, Deja. I took care of you, and you know that."

"J.R, I'm sorry. I guess I'm just stressing bills and stuff. I don't know. I just want the old times back."

"Dej, I just told you. I will go out and flip some weight for you so you will be straight for a moment."

"Okay, J.R. I won't ask you to do that. Just look out for me please."

"Dej, don't I always? Look, here is a little something to help you out. I got some stuff in the works don't worry. Just know I always got your back."

"Thanks, J.R."

He gave her some money and played with the kid for a little while. He then left because he had other errands to run. J.R was thinking about these guys that he used to sell pounds of weed to, and he remembered that they used to do music or have some dealings with some music business. So he rolled past their spot and they kicked it for a few.

"Yo, what's up? Y'all remember me?"

"Hell yeah, nigga. You had that good smoke. How could we forget?"

"Yeah, I did, but I ain't with that no more."

"Yo, what do you mean? You had the good stuff and pounds on demand. That sucks. I could have paid you some good money for a pound right now."

"Well, it ain't why I'm here today. I remember that you used to deal with some music cats. Can you hook me up with them?"

"Well, it ain't nothing right now. I think they have an independent label. I know they have a recording studio in Chesapeake or Newport News. Other than that, there's not much I know. I can give you a card, and you can call."

"Aiight, bet. Let me have it. Oh, and if I run across some good loud, I will get some to you."

"Cool."

He handed J.R a card that had Brian Bass and Ronald Record's names on it. He needed to look into these cats and find out what they knew and what was up with them. He needed to get Ron Ron back on the map and himself into some legit business. He talked to Ron Ron about meeting up with these guys and let him know he had been looking into another company to back his music. He had meetings with labels, and one after another, they kept turning them down. He finally got a meeting with Ronald Record and Brian Bass. He told Ron Ron, and he got excited. J.R was grateful for the meeting. He had been pushing for a while. and although his funds were not low, he really didn't want to keep going in his stash.

It was the day for the meeting. He went to pick up Ron Ron, and they both were very nervous. They parked, got out, gave each other a dap, and said a little prayer. When they walked into the office, the receptionist came to greet them. She said, "Mr. Record will be with you in a second." So they waited. They were thinking about all the other record labels they had been to were dealing with the former record label, and they had them blackballed and felt like this might be the same thing. J.R was thinking out loud, "What is the worst thing that could happen? Us back in the streets, selling drugs like before. So what? Let's take a chance." Ron Ron chuckled.

"Hey, you never know, but I actually never sold dope before," said Ron Ron.

"Maybe that was a good thing."

J.R just wanted a proper deal to showcase his and Ron Ron's talent. Before long, a man came to the door and said, "Bring them in please."

They were escorted into the office. The first thing J.R heard in the office was Ron Ron's first album playing. He was shocked. It looked as though they had done some research on them. They had actually been looking for them. It was like it was destiny for them to meet. They had already heard of Ron Ron, but not J.R. He let them know that he was a part of his team. They did not want to record new material yet. They wanted to take them on tour with the old songs. They started talking numbers and what cities they wanted to do for the tour. They didn't talk about providing money up front, but what they did say was that they would make money on the road. J.R was a little skeptical at first, but they said if everything goes as planned, they would get about $500,000 each after taxes. After the tour, they will get in the studio to work on new material. They started providing information about the company and letting them know that they were bigger than their previous record label. They let them know that they had financial backers. J.R was thinking they must be part of a major record label. What he didn't know is it was affiliates of the Italian mob from Upstate New York backing them. They needed a way to wash money, and the record label was the front for their operation. Everything would kick off in two weeks. They needed to get things in order because they would be gone for six months. J.R had a lot of money in the streets, and he needed to get that back since they weren't getting any advances from the record label. Ronald Record and Brian Bass kept in contact with J.R to make sure that he and Ron Ron were still on board and on track for the tour dates.

While chilling at the crib, putting in his new security system, relaxing, and drinking a beer, J.R got a text from Tianna. This was the text he had been looking for. Everything was coming together for J.R, he had a nice record deal and a bad chick checking for him and giving him the opportunity to check for her. Ron Ron was feeling better. Everything was going great. J.R and Tianna texted a few times. She told him a few things about her, and he told her a few things about him. J.R didn't tell her about his record deal. He wanted to see where her mind was at before he told her he was about to make it big in the music industry. He told her that he was a regular guy with a few small investments and that he owned a commercial cleaning business. The story explained the few dollars she saw him with and the nice car that he drove. Long story short, they chopped it up for a while, and the vibe was awesome. Days later, J.R went to see Deja and dropped her off some money, then he went to holler at the guys that asked about the weed. He set them up with a nice little situation. J.R told them to work with Deja. Deja was put in a position to be the middleman instead of J.R so she could make a little money to have in her pocket. J.R also put some guys in the mix to look out for her. If something happened to her, the guys were to take care of the situation immediately. Since J.R was going on the road, he wanted Deja protected. A few more days went by, and they were finally on the flight headed to Atlanta, Georgia. Things were about to take off.

The Tour

The plane ride felt like it lasted forever. Not that it was, but J.R hated planes. But he knew he had to do what he had to do. He even thought about taking on Ron Ron as a full-time artist and becoming his manager. He wanted to possibly some-day have his own record label. He was going to make Steph eat his words and regret following behind the major record label that didn't care anything about him. J.R felt like they built a family relationship and Steph ruined it. When the plane landed, they had to meet up with the promoter at the spot they were performing at. But first they checked into the hotel, showered, and then were on the way to see the promoter.

Instead of renting a car, J.R took an Uber. He charged his phone while texting Tianna, letting her know that he wanted to take her out on a few dates once he got back. They were on the road for six months. But they were going back home in between time to check on business with Deja and make sure her daughter was all right, as well as check on family and friends that he hadn't seen in a while. He wanted to let them know he was doing good and okay. Ron Ron didn't ride with J.R; he went ahead of him so he could go do a sound check. So as J.R got closer to the club, he got a text from Brian Bass. "We need you to pick up the bag from the promoter." J.R was thinking he was talking about the money for Ron Ron's show. So he was like, "Cool." J.R got there, and the lines were super long. They were not only there to see Ron Ron but a few other artists as well. They weren't on Ron Ron's level, but their buzz was pretty big. Ron Ron rocked the crowd, and they were loving him. Ron Ron had this underground following where everyone knew him even though he wasn't big on the radio. J.R was feeling good about the love that Ron Ron was getting from the crowd. They went backstage to get the back end money. Usually the money is received up front, but the record label set things up and they claimed they had good ties with this promoter so J.R wasn't tripping. The promoter handed J.R a big duffel bag with, like, $250,000 inside. J.R was like, "What the fuck is this all for us? Do I take this back to Brian?" There is no way all of this was for them. Something ain't right. J.R took the promoter to the side. "You gave us too much."

"No, actually I'm half short. Once they deliver the rest of it, I'll have the rest of the money."

"Deliver the rest of what?"

He was like, "You haven't talked to your people?

J.R was looking like he was lost. He needed to get Brian on the phone. J.R hit up Brian. "Yo, Brian, what's up? What's the deal? This cat just handed me a quarter of a million dollars, talking about how he will have the other quarter when you make the drop-off. What drop-off is he talking about?"

Brian basically said, "Look, man, I'm going to keep it real with you. We have been watching you on the street for a long time. The streets talk. We knew of Steph. We knew of you, and there's a lot of heavy people connected in the game that you were connected to. We knew you were dealing with Ron Ron and the label situation and how they got him black balled right now. So we figured we get him signed that way we could get you, and we could do business. I know you got other connections. You know how to handle this work like a magician. We put Ron Ron on the road and you handle this money. What do you say?"

J.R said, "That's what the fuck I got out of the game for: to get away from shit like this, man. No, I don't want no parts of this."

Ronald Record and Brian Bass basically said, "Take it or leave it. The guys we work for don't really care about the music for real. This is their way to clean up their money. Either you with it or not. We can make you a very rich man, if you make this happen for us. When the tour is over, we can hit you with like $750,000 cash tax free. What do you say? And this has nothing to do with Ron Ron's show money. This is added. You will get it at the end of the tour. What do you say?"

J.R sat there. Then he hung up. He didn't know what to say. The one thing he was running from, he ran right back into it. He was thinking this was an opportunity to be legit and get the fuck out of the way. It was like J.R was thinking that he couldn't get out of the game for nothing. How did he end up in this situation? Now he was selling dope for somebody else. He didn't know if they were working for the feds, or if they owed people or got people out to kill them or what. He didn't know what he was in the middle of. Nevertheless, J.R, being who he was, the hustler and businessman, had to strategize and play it smart. The same way they are trying to use him, he had to use them. J.R didn't let Ron Ron know what was going on because he didn't want to discourage him. Ron Ron already got discouraged while working with Steph. When he turned his back on him, even though it wasn't personal, Ron Ron took it as such. J.R had hyped Ron Ron up, being that his girlfriend is pregnant. He felt that this was an opportunity to make it big. This situation might take Ron Ron determination down to zero. In the meantime, J.R wanted to build up Ron Ron and put his confidence level to a new high. J.R had a new motivation. Every city they went to, they would hit the studio and make fresh music and take the opportunity to make this money. At the end of this tour, J.R would take the $750 grand plus the tour money that he and Ron Ron would make to start his own record label. He wanted to call all the shots and make things happen for him and Ron Ron. This was the new plan. Night after night it was the same thing. They would drive all day. At night or every other night they pulled up in a different city and met with the promoter. The promoter took the bag and gave J.R a bag. Then he would give that bag to whomever he had to give it to. Ron Ron performed his show set then they would leave and go straight to the hotel, get some sleep and do it all over again the next day.

EPISODE 4

Visiting Home

One weekend, they flew back home to Virginia to see their loved ones. Ron Ron got to see his pregnant girlfriend. J.R went to see his mom and li'l sister, as well as check on the situation he had set up for Deja. He went to his house, relaxed a bit, took a shower, and made some calls. Then he bounced and hit this li'l spot, MP Island Cafe, in Norfolk to have a few drinks and get his mind right. A few people walked up to J.R to express love. They were asking if he is the one that was rocking with Steph on the music thing. J.R expressed, "Nah, I'm not really rocking with Steph like that anymore, but we are still cool, though. I got this little promotional thing going on now with Ron Ron. Nothing major or big, something to get him on his feet."

They were like, "Do your thing, man, hold it down. Rep the 757." That's what they planned to do. The next thing you know, J.R saw this bad ass chick walk in the building. Man, he was thinking like, *This gotta be meant to be. I met this chick in downtown Suffolk months ago at a gas station. I talked to her every night while I was on the road. I didn't even tell her that I was back in town, but she and her girlfriends walk into the same spot I'm in, at the exact moment that I'm here.* She was looking so good. He was tipsy as shit. He texted her phone like, "How are you doing? What's going on?." He just wanted to see what kind of chick she was. Was she a real chick or a lying ass chick?

She was like, "I stopped at MP's in Norfolk with my homegirls to get a few drinks and to relax." The first thing he did was smirk. She

16

was for sure a real chick. She could have easily texted him and said "I'm at home, chilling" or "I'm at work." She kept it real with, letting him know she wasn't on no fake shit. He appreciated that.

He texted her back, "Coincidentally, I'm here too."

She was like, "Really? Where are you?"

"I'm at the bar."

They hugged, sat, and talked and talked. One drink led to another and another. The next thing you know, they were on the strip in Virginia Beach, walking and talking. She told him about her future plans. He then started telling her about what was really going on with him, because initially he told her he had to go out of town to handle business, but he didn't exactly tell her it was the music business. He didn't want to make the first approach to be "I'm an entertainer and I'm about to make it big." He kind of let her know that he was doing okay, not as good as he was really doing or about to do.

She said, "I'm not even like that. I got my own money. I make my own chips. I got my own plans. Anybody that I end up with, it's going to be a fifty-fifty thing. You don't have to worry about that."

He was like, "I admire your style. You are a grinder. I admire how you look as well." She laughed. They had a nice talk and nice long walk. The weather was feeling amazing. One thing led to another. Next thing you know, J.R woke up the next day with his head spinning. *How much did I drink last night?* The sun was shining through the blinds. He looked over, and guess who was lying beside him? Damn, that body was bad, Tianna. He didn't even remember coming to the hotel with her. She was lying there asleep. She was still looking good and smelling good early in the morning, like she woke up and took a shower and put makeup on even though he knew she didn't.

Did we have sex last night? He didn't even have any condoms. She then started to wake up, and she turned and faced him. They stared at each other for a while. J.R looked at his phone and was like, "I gotta get out of here." He had to do a few things and catch his flight to the next spot. He couldn't tell her where he was going, but he had assured her that it wasn't a smash-and-dash type of situation. That wasn't his intention. He only came home for one day to see his people and hit the road again. She understood, though. She had the type of vibe where she believed him. And he wanted her to believe him because it was the truth. He really wanted to get to know her. Even though they had sex the night before, he didn't look at her like a hoe. They had been texting and talking for a couple of months. So it was not like he just met her yesterday and just fucked. They were both drinking and one thing lead to another. They enjoyed each other's company, and it happened. J.R was just mad at himself because he didn't remember what the fuck happened. But he was pretty sure it was amazing because Tianna was amazing. But long story short, he showered and got out of there. He had to meet up with Ron Ron and catch his flight, not even knowing which city they were going to. The next thing he knew, he was handing duffel bags over, and they were getting handed to him night after night. They had a little fun but mostly business, and he was cool with that. J.R just wanted all his plans to fall in place.

Back to the Tour

I t was the last show. Things were wrapping up with the promotional tour. Ron Ron got the opportunity to do more music. He did about four or five songs that night. J.R had to do this last drop off in San Antonio, Texas, and then he was out. Usually, Ronald or Brian would send certain people to pick up the money. J.R got used to dealing with them. On this night, they came themselves. They flew all the way out here from Virginia to meet with J.R in San Antonio. He wondered if they didn't trust him anymore. He didn't know what the case was. He had big duffel bags with about four or five million in them. They started checking the money and looking over it. J.R was thinking to himself like, *they can check whatever they want to check.* He flew a lot of money back already so they should know that he wasn't stealing from them. Brian then handed him a nice little small duffel bag and said, "Here's 150 thousand."

J.R said quickly, "This must be the back end for a show or something."

But Brian replied, "This is the money for the work you put in."

J.R said, "What? A 150 grand? I thought y'all were supposed to give me 750."

They were like, "Change of plans. When we made that deal, I didn't get the okay from the bigger bosses. They felt like you were Already getting paid from Ron Ron shows and 150,000 was fair."

J.R was thinking, *Fuck all that.* When a man gives you his word on something he gotta honor that word. Long story short, J.R got tempered up with his hands on his waist. Going for his pistol, he pulled it out and said, "Where the fuck is my money at? Fuck the contract. Fuck the label shit. I want my bread not now but right now!"

Brian Bass was like, "Whoa, whoa, whoa, easy. This not our cash. We are just the overseers. This is the Italian's money and drugs. We work for them, and you work for us."

J.R then quickly pulled out his pistol and aimed it at Brian Bass. The overly vicious bodyguard that was with Brian Bass pulled out his gun aiming it at J.R. That's when Ron Ron pulled out his. The next thing you know; everyone was spitting at each other. They were behind chairs, couches, and tables. All you could hear was gunfire. The next thing you know, Brian was hit. He was done. The bodyguard he had with him was done. J.R saw the promoter get hit; he was done. Long story short, after about twenty seconds of straight gunfire between all of them, Ron Ron was good. J.R was good. Everybody else was hit. Ron Ron was looking at J.R and vice versa. "Did we just kill these niggas?"

"More or less." J.R was thinking about those big-ass duffel bags on the ground full of four or five million dollars. J.R was like, "What the fuck are we going to do? We can't call the police. It's a whole big drug transaction." Not only did they have the four or five million in cash, they also had the keys to the van or the bus that had the work in it for the next drop-off. "You know what, Ron, man. You are not going to like this, but we gotta go." They took the duffel bags and threw them in the van and got the fuck out of there. The next thing you know, his phone started blowing up. All types of numbers kept calling. When he answered, he was getting all kinds of death threats. He responded, "See me when you see me out." He threw the phone and kept going.

Coming Together

J.R and Ron Ron drove all night with really no direction of their next move. They continued to drive when the sun came up. After about twenty-seven hours, they hit the Virginia state line with a van full of drugs and five million dollars cash. They were really relieved that they did not get pulled over with all of that weight and money on them. But immediately, J.R had to make a phone call to a certain person that he didn't want to. It was the same person that he was trying to prove wrong, and that was Steph. Steph answered, "Wassup, make it quick. I'm in a studio session." J.R started explaining everything frantically. Steph then said, "Woah! Woah! Slow down. You're talking too fast."

J.R then said, "We are basically on the run from some people we were recently doing business with. It's too much to explain, but things got out of hand for moral reasons and I had to handle it. Long story short, we got their money and a lot of drugs. We really do not know the rest of them, but they are based out of New York and we just need to lay low for a while until I figure out who we are up against. Besides that, I got to get this work off and take this money and do something with it. It's been a minute since I was in the game And I'm really not trying to deal with anyone that might be doing business with these people. They'd probably set my ass up and walk me right into a room with them. I need to holla at you about some of your old plugs."

Steph was like, "No, man, I told you a long time ago I don't fuck with none of that shit."

J.R argued with Steph, telling him, "This is my life right here. It's not the time to teach me a lesson. Come on, my nigga."

Steph was like, "Aight, man, chill out! chill out! Cool! cool! I got a dude I use to fuck with back in the day—Billy from Brooklyn. He moved to Virginia when he was in his twenties. He made a lot of money with me in the streets, but Billy was different from me. I was the type of cat that took my money and bought a lot of cars, shined on the streets, and got bigger and bigger. Billy got bigger as well. He took a lot of his money and washed it. Dude got truck, furniture, and all types of businesses. He has a legit way to buy homes and things like that. He got a big-ass beautiful house out in Harbour View in Northern Suffolk. I'm going to holla at him and see what's good. You get that work off, get the rest of that money right, and I'ma try to connect you with him. This dude is pretty big, probably twice as big as I was before I left the game."

New Game Plan—Part One

Steph got in contact with Billy. He told him he wanted to have a sit-down. Billy said, "Okay, cool." As soon as he saw Steph, he said, "I knew you would try to crawl back into the game."

Steph said, "Nah, this isn't for me, man. I want to talk to you about my nephew and see if you can do business." Even though J.R wasn't Steph's nephew, he saw him as one. J.R looked up to Steph, and Steph cared about him. That's why he wanted to pull this string for him. To be honest, the reason why he wanted to set J.R up with Billy was because of his ties in New York. Billy had a lot of power. He knew that if he set J.R up with Billy and he was earning Billy a lot of money, he wouldn't let any harm come to J.R. Steph knew this whole situation could kill two birds with one stone. J.R wouldn't have to worry about the mob guys. He knew Billy would teach J.R a lot. He would teach him about washing money and investing his money.

Billy, Steph, and J.R had the sit-down. They were introduced and got acquainted. Overall, through the conversation, Billy was with everything. Recently, one of Billy's highest earners got locked up, serving about twenty years. He really needed to fill that void. From what Steph said, J.R would be that void. J.R really knew what he was doing, and he had some money already. He was ready to get things started. Billy basically told him that he needed a fast earner that was going to bring him money on a regular basis and have the mind-set of building at all times. J.R agreed even though he wasn't sure if he could do everything that Billy broke down to him. J.R never had the quantities of drugs that Billy said he would supply. But J.R was who he was, so he was going to make it happen.

Meanwhile, while this is going on, Ron Ron was pacing back and forth in front of his girlfriend's mom's house not wanting to go inside. He was thinking, *If I go in, what am I going to tell her? The record deal thing is all fucked up. I didn't really make any money on the road. I really don't have a game plan for what is next.* As Ron Ron paced, trying to think of a lie his phone rang. J.R was calling him to break the news. "Didn't I tell you I was taking care of the situation. Don't worry about nothing."

Ron Ron was like, "I don't know what you brewed up, but we are sick of struggling and living in her mom spot, plus the baby on the way. I thought if I hit the road and got that promo tour money, I would come back and get us a house."

J.R assured him that he had nothing to worry about. "I'm about to do some investments with that five million that we took from the Italians. I'm taking three or four hundred to get you a comfortable house. I want you to take a million and do some investing in some properties. Look for some barbershops and hair salons. We are about to make some real moves."

Ron Ron was thinking at the moment that this could work. "Cool."

J.R advised, "Tell your girl that we got some money off the tour. The record deal didn't work, but with the money that we made, we are going to invest it. We are going to become full-time investors. We are going to open up businesses and start jobs in the area." Ron Ron was with it, but what he didn't know was that J.R had it set up to move more drugs than he ever did in his life and that Ron Ron would basically wash it through legitimate businesses. This was the game plan. J.R had to strategize. He couldn't just move all this work in Suffolk. He had to reach out and expand all over the 757.

New Game Plan—Part Two

The first thing J.R did was go to downtown Suffolk to see a few people who used to move work for him back in the day. He didn't come at them about drugs right off the bat. He wanted to test their temperature, to see how they were doing. They were not doing so good. Apparently, when J.R got out of the game, the streets dried up. At that point, no one had a plug to bring in the type of work that was needed. When Steph left, the same thing happened, but J.R was there to take over the torch. After J.R left the game, no one stepped up to carry the torch. Cats were going out of town or nearby cities to get whatever product that they could to try to keep things going. But the streets were frustrated. It was really no big action, so most of them fell off. When J.R realized what happened, he said, "Yeah, check this out. I got a proposition. I'm about to make this major move, and y'all two will be in charge of this city, including Deja. But I'm only hitting her with weed. I'm throwing y'all the pills, coke, dope, and lean big boy level. So you gotta put a team together. It's not like before when we was small-time. You need lookouts to watch for police and niggas trying to rob the stash houses. You need a bunch of shooters, runners, and corner boys. Y'all need a main stash spot for every hood. I'm putting this together by structure, and we are going to run it like a Fortune 500 company. Now, things might not start off the way you want, but things will continuously grow over time. Just get your people together. I have nothing to do with how much you pay them. As long as I get my money, everything is good. We friends, we go back a long way, but this is business. So that friendship shit is out the window the second I put that work in your hands. If anything goes wrong, I have to treat it like business. I'm telling you this up front so there will be no mis-understandings. You feel me?"

They responded, "We feel you."

J.R responded, "Cool, it is what it is. I'm going to holla at Deja, sit down with her, and go from there." J.R got back in his car and peeled off. As he cruised through the city, he was in deep thought. *Damn, it's crazy how I grew up in this town. Things weren't the greatest, but then I met Steph and came up in life. I thought to myself, it can't get any better than this. But dammit, I was wrong. It took me to get out of my element and do the music thing to realize how much bigger life could be. I traveled the world and met an amazing woman, Tiana, that I haven't talked to in weeks. I met people in different states and countries. I tapped into different situations that caused my mind to grow. The point is, I am back where I started, but with a bigger impact and a bigger vision. If I do everything the right way, this could be lucrative for all our family, friends, our kids, and grandkids. This is the plan.*

EPISODE 9

Putting the Pieces Together

Now that J.R got everything planned and situated in Suffolk, he was then off to the next few cities: Newport News, Hampton, and then Portsmouth, where he put his boy Li'l Pat in charge. Then he went to the beach with Ron Ron people from out of Twin Canal Village. Then they went to South Norfolk in Chesapeake. J.R even expanded outside the seven cities in Smithfield and Franklin with a few dudes he knew that was about getting money. He bought Ron Ron and his girl a nice house in Lynnhaven. But for himself, he kept the same one he had in downtown Suffolk. But he also got a condo out in Williamsburg where he stayed the most. He didn't want to be in his hometown a whole lot where many knew him or of him. He wanted to be off the radar as much as possible. J.R barely trusted anyone. The only reason he trusted Ron Ron was because he didn't have any ties to his drug operation. Eventually, he would tell Ron Ron everything about it. Everything was going good.

The only problem J.R had was when he was trying to make moves out in Norfolk, he ran into a brick wall, and that was old head Rick from Reservoir. He was an old school guy stuck in his ways and did not want any part of J.R's movement. Rick was the man in Norfolk back in the '80s and '90s. He got locked up in 2001. He did a long stretch. When he got out, he wanted his territory back. The only difference was, when he got out, the streets was not the same as when he went in. There were different young faces, prices, and the game was different, period. So what he did was put on his nephew

27

LB. His family called him LB, but the streets called him Beezy. He basically was running the city for Rick. And Rick still scored from the same plug from years ago before he did his prison stint. But now J.R was trying to network with Rick to expand his movement and get that Norfolk money, which was one of the biggest markets in the 757, but Rick wasn't letting up. J.R sent his people to talk to Rick, but nothing was accomplished. He declined the whole offer. "You not taking over nothing in my city."

J.R sent back a response: "I'm not trying to take over nothing. I'm trying to make you richer and the whole city eat better." But Rick refused it. He wanted to keep his situation the same. So J.R had to strategize. He saw an open hole. Beezy was working for Rick all this time and not going up financially, for real. He was making some okay money. He had a nice apartment with a Mercedes and maybe about two or three hundred bands in the stash, but he wasn't getting nowhere near the amount Rick was getting. Beezy was the one running the show for real. His girlfriend did hair and was a manager of a hair salon in Ocean View called the Braid Bar. That was J.R's open hole. And he took advantage of his opening. He went to talk to the owner. After a few weeks of negotiations, he eventually convinced her to sell him the salon and kept Porsha, LB's girlfriend, as active manager. This would be the beginning of him being cool with her, so he could end up talking to Beezy about cutting Rick out the equation and working with him and adding to his empire. So without Beezy, what would Rick do? He would not be able to move the way he was doing at this point, and J.R would make Beezy ten times richer.

EPISODE 10

Sweet Talking

J.R was headed down Tidewater drive in Norfolk on his way to the tunnel to get to P-town to holla at Li'l Pat about some business. He got a call on his phone from Tianna, but he hit decline fast. He was avoiding her since he got back to Virginia. Tianna didn't know about the whole shootout situation or about J.R getting back in the streets. The last time he talked to her was after he left Virginia and went back on the road. He didn't really know what to say to her. Since he declined her call this time, she sent him a nasty message basically saying, "Damn, I didn't want to believe this. I thought you were a stand-up guy. I see you full of shit like the rest of them." As he was driving at this point, he was going through the downtown tunnel heading into downtown Portsmouth, looking at the text like *Damn, this is not me. I don't want to give off the wrong impression. If she came around me now, she would clearly see what I have going on. But you know what, fuck it, it is what it is.* Then he thought, *She won't know because I got other things going on besides this drug thing.* J.R didn't want Tiana involved because of the beef with the cats from New York. He didn't want her around while this was going on. But everything was working out because he was also making legal moves and money that he could show her.

By this point, he was halfway through Portsmouth totally forgetting to stop at Lil Pat spot and heading to the Suffolk line. Thinking it was time to face the music, J.R called Tiana. She's like,

29

"Fuck, nigga. Damn, do you see me as a ho or something? I give you myself and you stop talking to me."

J.R was like, "No, no, no, no, it's not like that. It's not like that. I have been going through a lot the last couple of weeks. I was going to call you, but I had to make sure it was the right time. I look at you special, and I didn't want to put you in any bullshit. I could have easily called you or sent you a text, but that's not how I operate, I don't want to be messy, and I don't want to tell you no mess. The only reason I'm calling you now is because I don't want you to think I'm bullshitting you. It's the honest truth. What can I do to make it up? I want to see you again. I want to take you on a date. I want us to talk and put you on to everything that's going on, you know."

Tiana said, "I don't know. I don't know." She took a second. "All right, I'm going to give you another chance. We are going to talk this out."

J.R said, "Thank you. Thank you. I appreciate that. Let me hit you back. I got some important business I am about to go handle. I will call you soon."

She said, "Cool boo."

The Bud Setup

As soon as J.R hit Suffolk, he went to see Deja. She screamed, "Hey, boy I missed you!"

He replied, "You don't miss me that much. You just love all that money I'm putting in your pockets." Deja started laughing. J.R then said, "How is baby girl?"

"She is with my mom right now. I'll make sure I bring her to see you or set it up for you to see her. She misses you too."

"That's what it is, but yo, I got another situation with a new plug. I'm only getting a shipment once a month, but it's extra heavy. I hit up the plug I got for the weed and negotiated a whole new deal. So it's two different plugs. You are in charge of the weed out here as part of my green team, where y'all will handle all the bud. I got a person in every city that's responsible for moving their share weekly. I'm getting about a thousand pounds of high grade and a thousand pounds of mid grade every re-up. Big-boy level, can you handle that?"

She quickly replied, "Can I? Damn right."

J.R then said, "Cool" and hugged and kissed her on the cheek. "We back baby."

J.R hopped in his car and hit the road. At this point, he had people moving the bud weight already. His li'l homies Chavez and Kiante from Norview were flipping fifty to a hundred pounds a week. His people in Chesapeake, Hampton, Bad News, and the Beach did around the same numbers. J.R wanted the green team to be a whole different organization than what he was about to do with Billy. He made it clear he didn't want to mix the two, but outside of that, he hit up Ron Ron and let him know they needed an accountant ASAP because there was a lot of money coming in and they didn't need no mistakes. He wanted all the taxes paid on all the legit business and everything took care of the right way. He wanted everything organized.

Norfolk Takeover

J.R went back out to Ocean View to meet with Porsha, Beezy's girlfriend. He broke down the move he was trying to make and let her know about Ron Ron, since he was in charge of the legal investments. "My business partner Duron Artist is going to be opening up a chain of barbershops and hair salons. I see you got your license to do hair and have experience managing a shop. I want you to run this shop for me out in Ocean View. From there, I need you to manage all of them. What do you think? It comes with a lot of advantages, as well as 10 percent revenue of every shop would be your salary as well as bonuses. Duron would be your contact for everything. The money comes through you, then through him. What do you think of that?"

She was so excited. "Really, you trust me like that?"

"Of course, this is business. I have to trust someone. I don't know anything about doing hair. I am a businessman. Hair is your thing. I'm thinking about a unisex thing going in some of the shops. Some can be all hair, some can be all barbers. What do you think?"

She said, "Yeah, it sounds nice to me."

"Cool, I got Duron doing some deals in Portsmouth and Virginia Beach right now. Of course we got the shop in Oceanview, but I'm trying to open shops all over the 757. I want to make you a big businesswoman. I want you to be huge. I don't see a ring on your finger. Do you have a man?"

"I do."

J.R said, "I don't want you to think that I am trying to push up on you. I only asked you that for a reason, because I don't want to step out of my boundaries. You got a man, and I'm asking you to do all these important things. I don't want him to feel any type of way."

She was like, "My man is a businessman too."

"Yeah, what does he do?"

She looked real hesitant, like she didn't want to say. "I don't know if I can talk about this."

"Yo, holla at me. Me and you are about to be like sister and brother now. We about to do big business. I'm about to start making you a lot of money. When you doing business like this, we as black people need to stick together. Make sure we stay on our p's and q's. We gotta be honest with each other. I'm talking about real honesty."

She said, "I want to be really honest with you, because if we are going to be doing this business thing, I need you to know a little bit of what I do outside of hair. I'm going to be a hundred percent straight with you. My man sells drugs. He get big money. I don't want him to feel some type of way about me doing business with you, thinking me and you messing around."

J.R laughed. "Oh yeah, he does? What a coincidence. Maybe we about to be successful for real, because I do all types of things. Like I said, you think I'm opening up all of these shops because I was born with a silver spoon in my mouth? I'm doing big things, and drugs is one of them as well. Maybe me and him can connect. As a matter of fact, the way I'm setting you up with these shops, I got setups in all types of businesses. Maybe me, you, and your man can sit down to talk and come up with something huge."

"I don't know, maybe. I'll mention it to him."

"That's all you have to do. I'm here to make everyone rich. I'm pretty sure your man is making big money in these Norfolk streets. He's from Norfolk, right?"

She said, "Yeah."

"How about he get that money worldwide? That would be awesome. Even in this town, I can make him three or four times richer."

"Yeah."

"Holla at him about that. I'll get back with you. No pressure. I need you to meet my boy Duron so y'all can negotiate these shops, and we'll go from there."

"Cool."

"Bet." He gave her a hug. J.R hopped in the car. He had a bunch of running around to do. He called to make reservations at a hotel for the night; he was getting tired. He had been moving nonstop. Now he was on his way to meet Billy. He hasn't had rest in seventy-two hours. He was juggling this person and that person. It was well worth it since he had to make this money. The only way he could do it was to work hard and build his whole grind up. He had several people to go see. He had to go to Portsmouth and see this guy named Steve who hadn't paid him yet.

EPISODE 13

Building Umbrella

The first thing he did was call his homeboy Dre. He picked him up, and they went to Steve's spot. J.R parked on the side street and got out of his car. Dre cocked his gun back, and they walked toward Steve's door. J.R knocked on the door. Dre went to the back door with a big pistol in his hand. J.R didn't have a weapon; he didn't want to seem like he was coming as a threat. He had a nice little threat waiting at the back door for him, though. Nobody opened the door. Cool, they went to the side window, broke it, lifted it up. and hopped in. J.R got in there and heard moaning sounds in the back. He was like, "What the fuck? This nigga in here smashing. Fuck that." They kick the bedroom door in. J.R was like, "Yeah, nigga. Where my money at?" The cover lifted up, but it wasn't Steve. It was another dude smashing this little hood chick.

The dude was like, "What the fuck y'all doing?"

Dre put the gun to the nigga's head and J.R yelled," where the fuck is Steve?" this nigga owe me 'bout two hundred bands, man. I left town, and it's been a few months. I'm back now. I ain't seen this nigga. He ain't called me or anything. I shouldn't be explaining this shit to you, but if I want my money, I got to explain something."

The dude said, "Listen, my name's Revell. Steve is locked up. He got locked up two months ago, man. He said that he got this work from a guy he knew back in the day. He hit me with it. He told me I have to do some time so I need you to flip this work. He had me set up with the connect that you had him set up with, and I have

36

been picking it up and making money ever since. I didn't know who to give the money to. He's locked up, and I don't know you."

J.R said, "Yeah, show me something. Show me some bread then. He owe me like two hundred at this point."

Revell said, "I got you." He showed J.R the money. "I even got some bud here from the last drop off."

"Yeah, you moved all this yourself?"

Revell was like, "Yeah I'm doing my thing. Why do you think this hoe on my dick like this?" They all started laughing. "You see I'm getting pussy. I'm getting money."

J.R said, "Yeah, as a matter of fact, Revell, I got a proposition for you then. I know that I don't know you, but we can get well acquainted. This whole gun thing, don't take it personal. I had to do what I had to do. This bullet was for Steve, and for the record, I never liked Steve in the first place. The thing is, I was going to set Steve up because he is a clown-ass nigga. The only reason why he needed you to grind this bud for him was because he planned on running away with my money, anyway. I never rocked with this dude. He did some foul shit to me back in the day. I vowed to get him back. I made him think everything was okay. I was going to bust his ass after he made me a couple million. You know what? How about we leave him in jail for now? When he gets out, we'll take care of him."

Revell was like. "I never liked him either. I was homeless at the time, and this dude stepped in and gave me a place to stay. He had me flipping bud for him and gave me something to eat. I have been staying at his crib, so I got cool with him, but he can't be trusted. A real clown. I never liked his bitch ass."

"I know you stay in Portsmouth, I already got some people moving hard work for me out Portsmouth, but the way you are flipping this bud fast like this I think Ima put you in charge of the weed in this area. Can you handle a hundred pounds a week?"

Revell said, "What? Can I? Nigga, the re-ups I was getting from the dude you had set up wasn't giving me nearly enough. I needed way more than twenty pounds, and he wasn't coming fast enough."

J.R said, "Well, he's coming fast enough now because I'm back. The reason I had it set up like that was because I wasn't around. I didn't want to put too much out here. That would have been too much money coming through that I couldn't see. I had it coming small, so I could control it. Now that I am here, he'll send as much as I need him to send. This is the plan, man. I am going to get with you in seventy-two hours. Be ready. The two hundred bands that Steve owed me are yours. It's an advance. Get yourself a new spot, and get out of this piece of shit crib right here. Get yourself some new clothes and a new whip. When Steve comes back, take his ass out."

J.R knew right then and there that Revell was a rider, a go-hard street dude, and a loyal street soldier. He needed people like that on his team. Having Dre and a slew of other guys that would kill for him at will was a plus, but he saw something different in Revell's eyes. The boy had a fire in his eyes. This dude wouldn't back down for nothing and was loyal to the end. J.R walked up on a gold mine for a soldier. He was about that money and would bust his gun.

EPISODE 14

Love in the Air

With that being said, as they left Steve's spot where Revell was staying J.R started to feel extremely tired than he was before. He's had business deals with Beezy's girl and Billy. He was collecting money that was owed to him and meeting with Deja, going to Newport News, picking up money, and dropping off more trees. J.R was basically tired at the end of the day, and not getting the proper rest will take you off of your game, man. But at the end of the day, he didn't want to break his promise to Tianna. J.R hit Tianna up and said, "What's going on? How are you doing?"

"I'm cleaning the house, and then I have to run a few errands."

"You know what? I miss seeing your beautiful face. I miss your smooth skin and nice smells. I want to take you out to eat tonight. I'm a little tired, but I want to make that move before I get some rest tonight. Have some dinner. Maybe we can negotiate our future."

"Future. Is that right? You see yourself with me?"

"Do I? I can't see myself with anybody else. You just too bomb, and I gotta have you."

"Ha ha."

"Nah, for real, though. I'm about to hit the spot, take a shower, and get my mind right. I'll maybe have a small drink and get dressed. I want to take you out to eat. It doesn't have to be anywhere fancy, maybe Texas Roadhouse out Harbour View or something. Just a little something if you with it."

"Of course, boo. I'm about to get in the tub. Get myself all nice and pretty for you, and we can do that."

"Bet that's what it is."

J.R hung up and went straight to the hotel. When he arrived, he turned the shower on, poured himself a drink, and sipped on it before he washed up and got himself together, followed by putting on his creed cologne. He grew tired with each step. He didn't let being tired affect him. He jumped in the whip and texted Tianna for her address so he could pick her up. When he arrived at Tianna's house, he was even more tired. J.R was at the point where he started swerving on the road while he was driving earlier. Nevertheless, he shook it off. Tianna hit J.R back and told him that she wasn't quite ready yet and she would leave the door unlocked for him to walk in while she was still getting dressed. J.R walked in and admired Tianna's spot. He wondered for a bit what she did for a living, but he didn't wonder too long on the subject. He took a seat to wait for his date. Tianna yelled from the back, "Hey, J.R. Is that you?"

"Yeah, it's me."

"Give me a minute."

When Tianna finally came from the back, J.R was slumped on the couch, super fresh. His gear was on point, and he smelled fantastic. Tianna thought to herself, *Damn he is so remarkable. He's smooth, handsome, and he's obviously about his money.* She tapped him on his shoulder. J.R responded, "Huh, my bad, my bad. How are you doing?" as he kissed Tianna on the cheek. "I got something for you." J.R pulled out flowers, old-school style. He always wanted to do that for a women.

He gave her the flowers, and she said, "Thank you. You know what, you look tired. I say let's not go anywhere. I am going to turn the TV on, and we can just relax. If you are hungry, I can whip up something for you."

"No, I promised that I would take you out to eat something."

"I don't care about that. The fact that you took the time out of a busy day, you're tired, and you still wanted to see me means everything."

"You sure?"

"Yeah."

J.R sat there while Tianna went to take off her dress to put on some comfortable night clothes. She went to whip something up in the kitchen. She came back, and they ate and talked. J.R fell asleep again because he was so tired. He woke back up, and to his surprise, it was to something he didn't anticipate. She was sucking the shit out of his dick, man. J.R was like, "Oh, shit. The fuck." This was that grade A quality, crazy dome. J.R was thinking, *Yes, she's a keeper.* She sucked J.R to sleep indefinitely. When he woke up, he was in her bed. He asked, "How the fuck you get me up here? When did I fall asleep?"

"Yeah, you were a party pooper. You fell asleep on me."

Tianna was already up cleaning the house, and she smelled so good. She was cooking food. J.R was thinking, *Damn, man, this is paradise. I'm loving this chick.* He got up. She had a hot bath waiting for him. He got in and relaxed as they were discussing this and that and getting to know each other more. It was a great vibe. It was just a great moment until it hit him that he had to go meet with Billy. He got up and put the same clothes that he wore the night before back on. He told her, "Look, I really don't have time to eat, but we really going out and have a little dinner."

"Cool, boo."

"I enjoyed my night with you. I plan on enjoying plenty more nights with you."

"Likewise."

He kissed her on the forehead, and he was out. As J.R was pulling out of Tianna's driveway, he was thinking that she might be the one. She was so bomb, pretty as shit, and was always smelling good. She was real. She was loyal. This was perfect for him. He was really feeling this. This was what he wanted. He could see her as his future wife.

EPISODE 15

The Unexpected

J.R was heading down Highway 58 almost at the 264 exit, heading to Virginia Beach. Usually he had to meet Billy at his Harbour View home in Northern Suffolk, or sometimes Billy would tell him to meet him at one of his nightclubs. This particular morning, he had to meet Billy at his beach condo. He was going through the downtown tunnel, and he thought to himself that he wanted to stop in Norfolk real quick to chat with Porsha to see if she got Beezy on board with the plan. As he was driving through town, by the McArthur Center and Tidewater Park, near the Popeyes and McDonald's, he realized it was a car behind him. He didn't think too deeply about it. He just kept driving until he got on Church Street over by Parkplace. He realized the car was still behind him, so he turned on one of the side streets and the car turned behind him. J.R was like, "What the fuck?"

The car then pulled beside him, and someone in the passenger seat yelled, "Yo, pull over!"

J.R kept driving. They were on the wrong side of the road, trying to get him to stop.

They said again, "Pull over."

He then rolled his window down, smiling. "Who you?"

"Don't even worry about it. Pull over."

"Cool, it is what it is." J.R pulled over, looked, and saw he had his AK-47 on his back seat. He grabbed his four pound out of the console and put it on his lap for them to see it once they walked up.

42

There were three of them. One stayed in the car while two walked up to his window.

"Yo, you J.R, right?"

"Yeah, who wants to know?"

"Look, man, we are Rick's people. He wanted to send you a message. He is not cool at all about you coming through his city doing as you please, and it has to stop now.

"Yeah, is that so? What exactly am I doing?"

"Trying to take over his territory."

Ha ha. "Man, I'm not trying to take over his territory. I got my own territory and plenty of it. All I'm trying to do is put money in his pocket."

"Rick already got money."

"No, Rick got chump change. He never had real money. You know what, that's none of my business. Tell Rick to do what he do. I'm out of his way.

"All right, cool, this is the final warning."

J.R laughed and turned his music back up, put on his cold black sunglasses, and peeled the tires in his Audi. He played cool, but man he was pissed off. He wasn't feeling that shit at all. This was the second time Rick came at him disrespectful. The first time, he denied his offer to get money and basically told him fuck you. Now he got someone to approach him. That's it, man. He was going to meet up with Porsha, but he was so furious at that point that he didn't even go. He hit the interstate and went to Billy's condo. Before he got there, he called Revell.

Revell answered. "Hello."

"Yo, I got a mission for you."

"What's good?"

"I will hit you with the details later."

"Say no more."

"That's what it is." They hung up, and he shot straight to Billy's spot.

J.R finally arrived at Billy's condo, and instantly he noticed a lot of nice cars parked everywhere. Billy had some type of luncheon or brunch going on. Everyone was dressed in business attire, drinking

Moet mimosas and eating all kinds of delicious food. It was a friendly laid-back environment. Billy approached J.R, shook his hand, and started introducing him to people. You would have thought Billy was the mayor or something while he was smiling and shaking hands and whatnot. Then he told J.R to follow him. They went upstairs to his office. Billy said, "Listen, I know I told you that the drop was coming in about two weeks, but there's a change of plans. It's going to be today." He rolled up the blinds, showing J.R six vans parked out back of his condo. "See those vans right there? They are full of grade A everything. Are you ready?"

J.R started rubbing his hands together, grinning and smiling like, "Yeah, it's on, man." Nothing but dollar signs were running through his mind.

Billy told him, "Look, bring your people here tonight to pick these vans up. Do whatever you have to do to unload your work. Make sure you bring my vans back within twenty-four hours. As a matter of fact, I will give you forty-eight. From there, I will just be waiting on my money."

J.R was still rubbing his hands together, thinking like, *This is it. This is it.*

Bossing Up

J.R texted Tianna a kissy face to her phone, knowing he would be too busy to spend time with her that day with the shipment in. He called Dre and said, "I need you to round up six people to pick these vans up. Now it's time to do the drop-offs." He hit up everybody: Li'l Pat, Puertorican Benny, all the boys, all the runners from Chesapeake, and NewPort News. He hit up all the top bosses to meet up with them to drop off the vans. When they were unloaded, Dre and his people picked the vans back up and took it back to Billy one by one. Everybody got paid for their services, and now the work was officially on the street. Although J.R had always been a boss, I have to say that this point was the highest level he ever reached, and things were about to change. He didn't feel comfortable riding around in his Audi by himself anymore, with all this attention on him with all the people and the work he was responsible for.

He told Dre, "You and Revell are about to be with me all day every day."

"That's what it is, man."

He hit up Ron Ron. "What up, boy?"

"Yo, what's good, man? I haven't heard from you in a week."

"Yeah, it's been a minute. How is everything going on that side?"

"Everything is good. I have been talking to Porsha. We got a few buildings, starting from the bottom up. We renovated a couple other ones. The barbershops and hair salons are going to be ready in the next month and a half. We are going to start hiring barbers, beauticians, and get it going from there."

"What about the real estate situation?"

"The real estate booming. We flipped a few houses. Buying up property in the 757, even a little in Maryland and the Carolinas."

"Cool, man, that's what it is. The car you are driving, the Cadillac, don't worry about that anymore. I just ordered you a nice stretch Mercedes. I got you a driver and a shooter."

"Yo, what the hell do I need a shooter for?"

"Look, man, you trust me?"

"Yeah, man."

"All right then, you're going to need one. This is big business, my boy. I need you in expensive suits to look the part, so make sure you go get fitted for a whole closet full. Nothing but the best. If you want to sip a little wine during brunch meetings, you can because you will have a driver. That's how I want it from now on. I'm going to do the same thing. I just ordered a nice Maybach. I also have a driver and a shooter."

"Yo, what about you? Are you okay?"

"Yeah, I'm good. It's a lot of things I got to break down to you that you don't understand right now. I didn't want to put that pressure on you. I know you just had your new baby girl. Congratulations on that, man. You and your girl are about to get married, and I'm paying for the wedding. It's on me."

"I appreciate that, man."

"Yo, everything is on me, man. I got somebody special that I want to introduce you to by the way. So that's what it is, man." They hung up and went on with their day.

The Hit

J.R went to downtown Suffolk and drove around, stopping through Jericho, Saratoga, South Suffolk, and Cypress Manor. He stopped by to see his mom and pops, then he went to kick it with his little sister briefly, not long, though, since he had a lot of work on the streets. He had to stay focused. He didn't want to get too caught up with relaxing. He was hanging out for a little while and helping out who he could help out. He paid a few people's rent, bought some groceries, and put a little money in everyone's pocket. He kept his people good. That was the kind of person J.R was. He never forgot where he came from. A lot of people got a lot of love for him, but a lot of people also feared him. J.R was a very dangerous guy, but the difference between him and other dangerous guys was, he was humble and far from a bully. But you better not play with him, though. He had a quick temper. He was getting better with it, though. This new level changed J.R in a lot of good ways. He wanted to go see Tianna, but he didn't have enough time. He wanted to sit her down to really let her know what's going on with him. He really didn't know how to say it. He didn't know how she would take it. That was just a thought in his mind. He had to shoot downtown Portsmouth real quick to get up with Li'l Pat to see how everything was going. Li'l Pat was his homey. That was his little brother; he really rocked with him. Li'l Pat was a hustling mufucker, though. He was out there doing his thing. He went to Effingham Street and met with him. Everything was cool; money was coming and fast. It was coming so fast. He was thinking about talking to Billy about dou-bling his supply, but he wasn't sure yet.

J.R called Revell. "Remember that mission that I said I wanted to put you on?"

"Yeah."

"You ready?"

"Yeah."

"Meet me in ten minutes."

He pulled up in London Oaks. Revell was smoking a blunt, sipping a little bit, and relaxing in one of the apartments that they stashed some of the work in. Revell had to go there and check up on everything to make sure nobody was trying to skim from J.R. That was what he did. He rode around town and checked on things. J.R soon would have him checking on things in other cities as well. But straight to the point of him going there, J.R was like, "It's about a nigga from downtown Norfolk, a nigga named Rick. Old head is supposed to be running the city. He really got his nephew Beezy doing it, though. But yo, this nigga disrespected me a couple of times. I went to put some money in his pockets and drop a bit of work on him, and he told me, 'Nah, fuck you.' I let that slide. That was a few weeks ago, but just yesterday, he had muh fuckas following me. They pulled up and basically gave me a warning that I can't be coming through the city and whatever. So I need you to take this nigga out."

Revell was like, "Say no more." That was what it was. The order was officially put out on old head Rick.

Meanwhile, out in Huntersville, Beezy was meeting up with Rick. He collected the money from each hood. Then dropped the money off to Rick like clockwork. It was their routine. He had about two or three duffel bags; it was a pretty good day. There was no telling how much money was in those bags. Rick got into his BMW 7 series, and he drove off, playing his old school music. He was cruising, not worrying about nothing because he was in his city. He had respect. He had been doing it for a long time, but he just got older and was slipping a li'l bit. He had no idea a car was behind him the whole time. He pulled up in front of his house, got out, and walked toward his house with the duffel bags. Before he could turn the key in the door, an AK-47 was lighting his ass up, and that was it. He was dead, and the car drove off. That was the end of old head Rick.

Celebration

J.R's organization was building strong and fast. He even had a name for it called Umbrella. Under the umbrella, there were different sections. You had the legit side, which was run by Ron Ron. Ron Ron was the boss. He was in charge of the accountants, the lawyers, and the developers. He was also in charge of all the managers for all the businesses. Even though J.R was the overall overseer, Ron Ron was the boss of that side. Of course J.R was the boss of the street side. In every city, J.R had a kingpin that he dealt with. The kingpins had someone under them called a lieutenant. The lieutenants reported to the kingpins. Each lieutenant had an underboss who worked for them. The underboss controlled the runners and the shooters. This was the chain of command for each city. The kingpins of each city met up with J.R once a week. He always had a round table meeting. One particular day, they met up with J.R at his condo in Williamsburg. J.R and the kingpins had a productive meeting. They squared away some situations and talked about the increases and decreases of money and supply. J.R wanted to have a nice night at the club to celebrate the success of the Umbrella. He rented out the Alley in Newport News. J.R expected everyone to show up to the celebration. He just had to fill a few voids as far as the Norfolk situation.

Later on that night at the Alley, the energy was awesome. The DJ was rocking with the music on point. Champagne, wine, liquor, and a lot of trees were flowing around the building. J.R hired a caterer to provide the food, and everyone was eating well. Everyone was having a good time and dancing. J.R invited Tianna. She was there and was looking pretty as ever. All his kingpins from each city showed up. It was a nice night. Ron Ron was there. Everyone was mingling and getting to know each other. It was a good vibe. Not everyone knew each other personally, but this was the beginning of a tight-knit organization called Umbrella that J.R was at the top of. Billy was not able to show up because of business he had to tend to in New York. Ron Ron even invited Porsha to the celebration. She was talking to someone as J.R tapped her on the shoulder.

"Hey, how are you? I haven't seen you in a while. I know you have been working close-knit with Ron Ron lately and not me. How is everything going?"

"Everything is great. Everything is awesome. How are you?"

"I'm good. Business as usual. What's wrong? You look a little down."

"I have been having a little issue in my relationship. My boy-friend has been a little down lately. Somebody killed his uncle. That was really who he did a lot of his business with, and he hasn't been the same since."

"Yeah, really sorry to hear that. Is he okay? Is business good?"

"Nah, not really on his end. Business is getting really tight. His uncle was really the person that set up his business and his product. My boyfriend has to really search around different cities. He's going out of town and paying higher prices. He is really stressed out."

"You know what, tell him to call me. As a matter of fact, I want to have a meeting with him to make sure he is good. He doesn't have to worry about that any longer."

"Really?"

"Yeah, I got him. I'm going to hook him up and put him on boss status. You think I made you a boss? I'm going to make him an even bigger boss. He has nothing to worry about. Condolences to his uncle. Sorry to hear that. Tell him to hit me up."

There it was. J.R was about to take over Norfolk as well. The rest of the night went well. Everyone partied and had a good time, as the night wound down. J.R left earlier than everyone else. He told them to continue and have fun. His driver pulled up with his Maybach along with his shooter for the night, Dre. Revell was out of town handling business for Umbrella. J.R and Tianna got in the Maybach and went to his condo in Williamsburg. Shortly after arriving and having a glass of champagne, J.R snuck up behind Tianna and kissed her with so much passion that she was breathless. J.R chuckled and said, "Breathe." He made love to her so good that night that she was moaning and speaking softly in his ear, driving him crazy with her sexy voice. He fucked the shit out of her so good that they couldn't get enough of each other. He switched his pace going from fast to slow and smooth to hard. He was driving Tianna crazy. J.R was doing his thing. Whichever position you could think of, J.R tried at least once. He made her feel like she was the love of his life. They both fell asleep from fucking all night long with a smile on their face.

Squashing the Beef

Meanwhile in Upstate New York, Billy had a meeting. He didn't tell J.R what the meeting was about. Apparently the same people that Billy got his supply from were the same people that supplied a lot of the Italian mob operations—drugs, guns, and whatever else they needed. The supplier was from another country. It was a very distant individual who was not seen very much but had ears to the street everywhere with resources and all types of information. Anyone that touched their drugs, they knew about it. Long story short, they knew about the situation with J.R. They also knew that he worked with Billy now. This was what the sit-down was about. Billy had great protection—a lot of hands, guns, shooters and killers everywhere. Billy has no ties with the Italian mob, but he was willing to protect his money. The people who supplied the mob knew that the mob was looking for J.R, but they also knew that Billy was supplying him. J.R is going to be one of Billy's biggest suppliers, which made Billy's money come faster, which made their money come faster. They called this sit-down, and since Billy was one of their biggest distributors, if anybody touched any of Billy's people, they were going to pull away from them. The mob felt some type of way. Their suppliers were willing to stop doing business with them just to make sure Billy was satisfied, and even though J.R was prepared for anything, Billy was still squashing the whole situation. They slapped a little tax on Billy. They felt like the mob should get reimbursed. Billy said, "I'm not reimbursing nobody because I don't have anything to do with that. You either want to go to war or let this go."

It sounded crazy, but it was business. The mob took a loss, and it was their own fault because they tried to shake J.R. They tried to trick him to do something without paying him. This was the result. He didn't steal from them. He took it after they tried to play him. As far as Ronald Record and Brian Bass, they were not part of the mob. The mob didn't care about them dying. They were only using them as well, and as a result, they died for their part in the situation.

The beef was handled with the Italian mob, and business was on point. Everybody was eating, but with success comes stress. The streets were in mayhem a little bit, with turf wars, drug dealers, and organizations that had nothing to do with J.R was beefing with J.R's people or beefing with the people that worked for the kingpins in the Umbrella organization. J.R had nothing to do with that, and that's why he had the organization. There were the kingpins, lieutenants, and the underbosses. They had the shooters to handle situations like that. J.R's job was to supply everybody. On J.R's end, life was lovely. He bossed up, and he was well protected. J.R went and got himself a nice-size yacht and flew to Miami with Tianna for a much-needed vacation to enjoy themselves. Ron Ron also went and brought his soon-to-be wife, along with Porsha and Beezy. They were enjoying themselves on that very nice yacht, drinking and just enjoying life.

Inspiration

J.R invited Beezy out to Miami with him to inspire him and show him the nice, expensive boat, the jewelry, and not to mention the grand opening of Club Umbrella Miami. Ron Ron had it scheduled for that night. J.R just wanted to inspire Beezy and not just throw money and drugs at him. He wanted to inspire him by showing him life outside of his city. He wanted to show him the levels of life beyond the few hundred thousand that he was worth. He wanted him to see that he could be worth millions, travel the world, and own businesses. Enjoying the moment, they sipped champagne. The women all looked extra beautiful. Everyone was smiling. Ron Ron was happy to be doing so much for his soon-to-be wife, Elmyra. J.R was thinking about business as usual. He was smiling, but he was focused. His brain was calculating numbers and what was going on here and there, but that was just how J.R was. Tianna was fine as wine, wearing a white two-piece bathing suit and sheer cover-up, white sunglasses, and white nails, looking extra beautiful. Everybody was having a good time. That night, everyone went back to their hotel to freshen up and get extra sharp for the grand opening. They all pulled up in a Maybach stretch limousine. There was a nice crowd. The club catered to the twenty-seven-and-up age group. There was none of the young stuff, no fighting, and no gang shit. It was a nice spot. They all walked in with their tuxedos and dresses on. There was a nice VIP section for the Umbrella crew. Ron Ron was there as well as Revell. Revell was not on the yacht that day, but he came that night along with Dre and Ron Ron's shooter. They followed them everywhere; they were never far behind. They had a good night. It was a way to inspire Beezy.

Later on that night, as the club was jumping, the crowd was loving it. They had a couple of speeches to let everyone know that everything was on them for that night; no one had to pay for anything. J.R slid to the side and tapped Beezy on the shoulder. "What do you think?"

"It's a nice club. I appreciate the invitation."

"Yeah, no doubt. But I'm talking about what you think. Can you see yourself with this? Can you see yourself with your own clubs? Can you see yourself with your own million-dollar boats, your own army, your women wearing anything that she wants, and unlimited jewelry? Can you see it?"

"Yeah, man. I'm loving this."

See, this was the whole idea. J.R wanted Beezy to see it from this aspect. He didn't just want to pull up on him in Norfolk and just drop drugs on him and show him a bunch of money because Beezy saw all of that before. He had seen levels of all types of drugs before even if he didn't have it himself. J.R showing him things from this aspect really had him inspired.

"Listen. I have a tight-knit organization. Not only is this club called Umbrella but my whole organization is also called Umbrella. It's like the whole planet can be ours right now. We can have anything that we want. There's no limit to what we can have. The sky is just the beginning point. Do you want a piece of this, man?"

"Hell yeah, I want a piece of this. Where do I sign up?"

"Ha ha ha. All jokes aside, I can put you in this situation. I know what you are used to, and I can escalate that whole situation much higher. All you gotta do is tell me that you are with it. We can make it happen right now."

"I'm definitely with it."

"Say no more. Enjoy your night. Drink as much as you want. Smoke as much as you want. Eat as much as you want. Enjoy your lady at that five-star hotel that I'm paying for. Everything is on me.

Don't worry about anything while we are here. If you want to go on a shopping spree to get fresh, it's all on me. I got you."

Beezy was loving it. As he lit his Cuban cigar, he sat back and sipped on his cognac, looking around like "I could see this."

"Sorry about what happened to your uncle. That's unfortunate. Sorry about his demise."

For a split second, Beezy was thinking, *I never told him about my uncle dying.* But just as quick as he thought it, the thought was gone. He didn't think too much into it. He just let it go and kept it moving. "I appreciate that."

That night, they partied and had fun as well as the next few days. Then they all had a first-class flight back to Virginia. Back to business. The only thing that was on J.R's mind the whole flight was to step his game up even more, because soon he planned to have his own private jet, like Billy, instead of catching commercial flights.

They returned to the 757 on a Friday. Friday was the usual day J.R held his weekly kingpin meeting. The meetings were usually just him and the kingpins, but today the lieutenants and underbosses was also invited. J.R's driveway looked like an exotic car dealership. A bunch of Porsches, Bentleys, Maybachs, a couple of Audis, and a few Lambos. J.R even had his new toy sitting pretty: his new sky-blue Wraith. Beezy pulled up in a brand-new corvette that J.R bought him as a welcome-to-the-team gift.

Everybody was seated at the round table, enjoying their brunch and talking among themselves. J.R was sitting at the head of the table as usual, looking very different than he normally did. Usually he would be wearing something like some nice Balmain jeans with the matching shirt, a lot of diamond jewelry, heavy chains, a Rolex watch, and a snapback ball cap. Probably some Air Max, New Balance, or Jordans; but on this day, he had on Christian Louboutin red-bottom dress shoes, an expensive button-up shirt, and slacks. He had a pinky ring, one diamond bracelet, and to compliment it, a $650 thousand Hublot wristwatch. Now at this point, J.R could definitely afford that on his own, but it was a gift from Billy for being his top earner among the people he supplied. Billy always spoiled his top earners with gifts and more opportunities to get more money. He felt that you needed to earn your way to higher mountains in this game, and if you prove yourself, he would show you more ways to advance.

As brunch was finishing up, J.R pulled Ron Ron to the side to finally explain everything to him about Umbrella. J.R had his personal attorney by his side the whole time. J.R introduced Stacey to Ron Ron and finally explained, "Look, my boy, I know you see money coming in out of control, and yeah sure we did open a lot of new businesses that are doing well. But the truth of the matter is, it's street money that's funding everything—all the nice cars, clothes, and great lifestyles we provide for our families. I have a three- to five-year plan to take us to heights we never could imagine before, so if you are with it, let me know." It didn't take J.R long to convince Ron Ron because at this point, there was no way he could turn away from this lifestyle. He was loving it, and his lady was very happy.

Since Ron Ron being on board was a go, J.R started the meeting by introducing his personal high-powered attorney, Stacey Bewcannon, to the crew. Stacey would be handling all of J.R's personal matters. She would work for him personally. She handled deals and made sure that he was getting his percentage properly on any ventures he had going on. Ron Ron would now be also a kingpin on the team. He would be in charge of all legal ventures of Umbrella. He would be the point of contact for legal advice, as well as lawyers that were on retainer. If the crew needed legal representation, they were advised to reach out to Ron Ron and he would set it up. Beezy was then introduced as the kingpin of Norfolk, but to add to that, he was also named J.R's personal lieutenant. When J.R was not available, Beezy would step into his place as the head of Umbrella. J.R based his decision on business, nothing personal. He didn't have to teach Beezy the way of the streets or how to handle himself as a boss. He was already the top earner of all of the kingpins. He was already running Norfolk before he became a member of Umbrella. Beezy was already a boss. J.R also named Revell as his personal underboss. The crew welcomed the new members and congratulated them on their new positions. For the next few weeks, J.R and Beezy got really close as he showed him the ropes of the organization so he would be up to speed when J.R needed him to step in.

Dre, who was the underboss to the kingpin of Suffolk, was the only one hating on J.R appointing Beezy as kingpin of Norfolk and his personal lieutenant. Dre felt like the position should be his. He felt as though because he was a longtime friend of J.R, he should have automatically been put in the position that Beezy was in. But in reality, Dre was a really good soldier, but he didn't really have boss potential. Yeah he and J.R did grow up together and were longtime friends. J.R still made sure he was in a good position and should not have any jealousy for the next person. J.R provided him with the home that he lived in with his wife. He had a safe full of money, and he really didn't have to worry about anything. Him putting personal feelings in the mix of business was clouding his judgement and allowing jealousy to fill his heart, and that was definitely never good for business.

EPISODE 21

Reflecting

As the weeks went by, J.R and Beezy got tighter and tighter. Dre was hating more and more as Beezy's power grew bigger and bigger in the organization. Everybody was getting used to him. His work ethic was starting to look a lot like J.R's. That was what J.R needed so he could leave him in charge as he went out of the country with Billy to Japan. But on the flip side of that, Ron Ron and his soon-to-be wife, Elmyra, was carefully planning their wedding that J.R promised to pay for as a gift, beginning with giving her $100 grand to buy dresses for her and her bridesmaids.

One night as Ron Ron sat in his San Antonio office, one of his many offices in the States, he got a call from Elmyra, who was in New York, shopping for dresses with her girls. She was very excited to speak with him. They hadn't seen or really spoken to each other in a couple days. Ron Ron, with his heavy workload, didn't seem as excited. And that quickly made her whole attitude change as she said, "Damn it's like that?"

Ron Ron stuttered, "No, no, no, bae, it's not like that. I'm just really tired. I promise in a few days, we're going to spend some time together and will make up for everything, okay?"

She hesitated. "Mmmmm, I guess."

Ron Ron knew she was pissed off as he asked her, "How is your shopping going?"

She said, "Everything is cool. We're in the bridal shop, sipping champagne and trying on dresses."

Ron Ron said, "Great, I hope you are enjoying yourself. See you in a couple of days. Love you." He gave her a phone Kiss.

She said, "I love you more. Talk to you later." They hung up.

Ron Ron sat there for a minute or two. As he looked at his watch, he realized how late it was getting. He quickly put all his paperwork inside of his briefcase and went to his car. Before going to the airport, he directed his driver to take him to the newest club that he opened in that area. The second he arrived, he approached the manager and promoter, checking on business. They assured him that business was booming. As a matter of fact, they anticipated to have a packed house that night as one of the biggest upcoming rappers in the game was going to perform. Immediately, Ron Ron noticed the rapper on stage doing sound check. He sat there in a daze for a minute, thinking about how much he missed doing music, but even though he was in a position of power and had plenty of money, music was still his passion. As a matter of fact, being in San Antonio made him realize that was the very place his music career ended, taking him back to a very dark night. But that moment would be short-lived as the manager approached him and handed him a stack of checks. He then shook his hand, and he left the building with his shooter close behind. His driver picked him up, and they headed to the airport.

EPISODE 22

Cause and Effect

The streets were getting wilder and wilder in the 757. The police were getting curious, wondering why the drug traffic was getting so heavy out of nowhere. This was the outcome of the Umbrella empire come up, and soon it would get even worse. But that was part of the game. It couldn't be stopped, only controlled to a certain extent; and that was why J.R grinded so hard outside of the drugs to make a legitimate life for him and the team and create a bright future.

As J.R prepared to go out of the country with Billy for about a month, he planned to leave all his responsibility to Beezy, and Revell would be lieutenant. Dre would be his underboss. J.R didn't have to worry about protection. Billy had plenty of security that J.R could use. Revell stayed in the States to look after Beezy as well as other things and missions J.R had him on at the time being. So with that being said, Billy and J.R took a very comfortable flight on Billy's very expensive jumbo jet to make moves. The rest of Umbrella carried on with business as usual.

Days went by, as Beezy was rolling through Norfolk dolo without his driver or shooter. He wanted to be low-key, and he wasn't driving anything fancy. He was in his Lexus LS with tinted windows and pulled up in Youngs Park Projects to go holla at some of his fam. As he got to the building, two of his li'l homeboys ran up to him. "Damn, LB, you been MIA for a few weeks."

Beezy replied, "Yeah, I know. I had some shit to handle. But what's up with y'all though?"

"We good. We good."

Beezy then said, "Aye look. I didn't forget about y'all. I had to make some moves to get more work. But now I'm good. I'ma have somebody drop some off on y'all in a matter of hours.

"That's what's up, bet. But aye. We know you know a lot of people getting big money. We was wondering if you knew somebody we could show our music to or if you were interested in putting some money behind us."

"I don't know if y'all are any good." He chuckled.

"Damn right, our shit fire. As a matter of fact, check out our YouTube page."

Beezy sat there for a second. "Bet, I'll see what I can do. But yo, answer your phone and be looking out for that work. I'm holla at y'all later."

Growth

Meanwhile, all the way in Japan, Billy had J.R sitting in an important meeting with a company that Billy was about to buy into that was really lucrative and had the potential to make billions. Billy wanted J.R to see another world outside of just normal mom-and-pop legitimate businesses like nightclubs, car washes, and so forth. He wanted J.R to become familiar with investing in and buying into massive companies that were maybe failing but could be reconstructed or rebranded and turned into a huge pay off for him with also generational wealth. As J.R sat and paid close attention to detail, he suddenly felt his phone constantly vibrating in his pocket. He looked and saw that it was Beezy. At first, his initial reaction was to just call him back after the meeting was over, but then he thought, *What if it was something going wrong with business?* He then excused himself from the meeting and took the hallway to call him back. "Yo wassup, you called?"

"Yeah what's good? You're busy?"

"Yeah a little, but wassup?"

"I just came up with a good idea to expand Umbrella and bring in even more money. I know you're all about branding and expanding, so peep this. I was out in Youngs Park and ran across some of my li'l homies that play the corner for me. They asked me to check out their music on YouTube. At first, I was like ok, with really no intentions. But when I went to make some moves later throughout the day, I seen some kids listening to music, and it seemed like everywhere I went, I heard the same song playing. Long story short, it turned out to be the same li'l niggas I told you that asked me to listen to their YouTube. They also asked me if I could put some bread behind them. With the way that song buzzing, I can vision some millions. What do you think?"

J.R's response was, "To tell you the truth, I feel that's a great idea, but it seems like every time I decide to get into music, it never ends up well. I'm not sure you or we should put a lot of money behind anybody, but I think starting a management company would be profitable. We sign a few artists to get them signed to a major label, get that machine behind them, and charge the labels top dollars for our management services."

Beezy replied, "I'm definitely with that!"

J.R said, "Cool, I will contact my attorney Stacey ASAP. She will get the process going to get an LLC for Umbrella Music Management, as well as get contracts pressed up for the artists. Since this was your idea, we can do a 51-49 split, and you can be in control. I also got a good contact for a major label through one of my old heads Steph that has his own company. He got a partnership with one of the biggest labels in the industry. If your li'l homies music's fire like you say, then I'm sure we can get them a deal."

Beezy was thinking like, *Damn, my nigga, we should have met earlier in life.* "You like the big brother I never had."

"I'm about to text Stacey, and she will contact you from there." As they ended the call, Beezy got into his car. J.R went back to the meeting and texted Stacey the details.

EPISODE 24

Business in Japan

As the meeting was ending, J.R contacted Stacey via text message about everything he and Beezy discussed. He was very interested in the idea, and to be honest, he still had a love for music. As the message went through to Stacey, Billy approached him, along with this gorgeous bad-ass chick that looked Asian but appeared to be mixed with African American. She was around five feet one or five feet two, with light-brown complexion and a body shaped extremely nice. She didn't have a big ass; it was a li'l handful, but it fit her just right. Her breasts were perfect. They were a little heavy, sitting up real high with her perky nipples showing very noticeably. Damnnnn! She caught J.R's attention immediately. He was feeling like he was about to burst through his slacks. He had to calm down and hold his composure. Billy introduced her to J.R and told him she was the active president of the company. "J.R, meet Yasmine. Yasmine, meet J.R Jones, my protege." He further explained to J.R, "I have other meetings to attend in nearby areas with other business to handle for the next few days. I want you to work closely with Yasmine to see if you can continue to go through certain things with her and my lawyer to close the deal." As Billy talked, Yasmine was staring at J.R as if she has never seen a man in her life. She was very attracted to him. She was impressed by his attire, his swag, and how he looked so young but seemed to have it all together. Yasmine was looking forward to working closely with J.R, and he was too.

As that moment was happening, back in the States, Tianna pulled in her driveway with J.R heavy on her mind. She missed him bad, so she was a little down that she couldn't be with him or see him at the moment. To keep it real, she was now in love with him. She got out of her nice brand-new Porsche that J.R bought her a week prior to him leaving for Japan. He cared about her a lot and would do anything to make her happy. She unlocked the door of her place and turned on her front-room light to see roses everywhere, balloons, and all types of gifts. On the coffee table was a stack of money so big it would make any female extremely wet, and that was exactly what happened. Tianna was missing J.R even more and was horny out of her mind for him. She didn't even open her expensive gifts, yet she just showered and used her toy for a while, thinking about J.R until she came two or three times as she fell asleep while holding the pillow he used the last time he was there because it smelled just like him. Her dreams were very sweet that night.

But J.R was in a whole different time zone in the world. It was around noon for him as Tianna slept the night away while he and this beautiful sexy woman he was with were on their way to eat and finish business. They arrived at a very nice expensive restaurant named Kitcho, which usually cost around $600 per person. That was no money problem for J.R. He was hungry as well as anxious to get to know more about Yasmine. His first question as they were seated was, "Do you have a last name?"

She looked, smiled, and said, "Of course."

J.R was like, "Well, you never told me, but if you don't want to, I understand."

She giggled. "Of course you can know my last name. It's Moon, which is a Japanese name." J.R was curious to know if she was mixed as she said, "Yes, I'm mixed with Japanese and African American. My father is black, and he is from Baltimore, Maryland, in the United States. He served twenty years in the army and was stationed here in Japan when he met my mother. They fell in love, but like most young people in love, things happened. Certain family didn't approve of them, etc., etc., and the list goes on. But as they separated in life and my father was then stationed back in the United States, my mother discovered she was pregnant with little ole me, and here I am." She winked and smiled.

J.R then said, "Yes, here you are, very beautiful." They went back and forth talking and complimenting each other. They were supposed to be discussing the deal for the company, but they were flirting the whole time. They went on for a while as they ate and after, until Billy's lawyer arrived and kinda changed everything. They were getting straight to business as they worked and worked on the deal, not exactly coming to a solution yet but close. They then parted ways for the rest of the day, but knowing they would see each other the next day. J.R went to his five-star hotel to shower and then check on business back home.

Before he called Beezy or Ron Ron, he hit up Steph. It had been a while since they spoke, actually not since Steph had connected him with Billy; but they were both busy so neither really had the chance. After three rings, Steph answered. "Damn, nigga, the last time you called me in the middle of the night some Italian muh fuckas was chasing you 'cause you had their money. Who chasing you this time?" He said it in a joking way.

J.R then realized that it was overnight back at home and immediately said, "Damn, my bad, Steph. I'm out of the country. The time zones are different. I wasn't even thinking about it."

Steph quickly said, "Nah, it's cool. I was just kidding, but what's happening though?"

J.R then replied in a joking way, saying, "Nah, nobody chasing me these days. If they tried, it would be bad for them."

Steph said, "Oh yeah? You must be bossed all the way up. That's wassup, but yeah, I wasn't asleep, anyway. I'm actually in the studio with this girl group I signed working on their next single. The first one didn't pop the way we expected, but hey, you know how the music business is."

J.R replied, "Yeah, but we need to talk."

Steph said in a sarcastic way, "What favor you need now?"

J.R said, "Nah, the way I see it, I'm trying to do you a favor."

Steph replied, "Oh yeah? Shoot."

J.R said, "As I see, your groups not exactly killing the billboards right now, but I think I got a solution for that. I got this group out in Norfolk, two young niggas that're buzzing heavy. I think this could be your next breakout moment. You should sign them and put that machine behind them. I'm sure that buzz is gonna turn into something ten times bigger. I can see it."

Steph sat for a sec and said, "Oh yeah? You think these boys got it?"

J.R replied, "Do they? Nigga, fuck yeah. They are the next big thing. You better get 'em now before Atlantic or somebody grab they ass up and you gon' be sick if that happens, my boy, trust me."

Steph then said, "Cool, send them to meet with me in two days. I'ma see what they about."

J.R said, "Say less." They ended the call.

J.R really had no idea if they were good or not. He was only taking Beezy's word on this. But the connection was done. All he had to do was call Beezy and let him know about the meeting as well as get them signed to the management company ASAP.

In the Absence of the Boss

Back in the 757, it was 3:00 a.m., and Beezy was in his Ghent condo hugged up with wifey, Porsha. Their relationship was kinda strained due to the lack of time spent. He was here and there, and Ron Ron had her all over the States handling biz as he opened a hair salon after hair salon. The chain seemed endless. They lay there, relaxed as she sipped on some wine, and Beezy then lit up a blunt of kush. They had just had sex, actually the first time in weeks, and now they were laid up relaxing as Beezy's phone rung. It was J.R. He answered immediately, thinking something was wrong; but when he answered, J.R calmly said, "You ready?"

Beezy said, "Ready for what?"

J.R replied, "To get this industry money, my nigga. I got a meeting set up with Cold Cash Records. My boy Steph told me to send your homeboys to him in a couple days, so if they buzzing like you say they are, then shit about to be on for them."

Beezy, very excited, said, "Bet" as he exhaled the smoke from his blunt.

J.R then said, "My attorney, Stacey, should have the contracts for them to sign for management before the end of the day tomorrow. So make sure they sign those before they sign any deal with the label. We gotta lock them in first."

Beezy said, "Understood!" Beezy was so excited after he and J.R hung up. He fucked Porsha two more times before they both fell asleep.

That was all good on Beezy's end, but about fifteen minutes away from him in P-town, out in Lincoln Park, two dudes were getting pistol-whipped badly. Apparently they got caught trying to break into one of J.R's stash houses, and Li'l Pat's underboss gave the order for two of his soldiers to beat the shit out of them until they told them who sent them to do that shit. But they were taking their beating and not talking. The lieutenant was contacted immediately, and he called Li'l Pat to see what he wanted done. Li'l Pat was pissed that he had to get out of his bed in the middle of the night. He had two bad-ass janks laid up with him. They were knocked out, asleep. He told his lieutenant, "Don't kill them until you find out who was behind this, so stop beating them before they pass out." Li'l Pat wanted to resolve this issue without J.R finding out. He told his lieutenant to hold on to the niggas they caught and that he had twenty-four hours to find out who was trying to come at him. They had a low tolerance for shit like that in the Umbrella camp. There were consequences for every action. They had to set examples around the city to make sure this shit never happen again, starting with the niggas who were plotting on him. Li'l Pat said, "Don't call my phone until you find this nigga."

The lieutenant responded, "Enough said."

The streets were getting way out of control. At this point, J.R was getting three times the supply from Billy as he did originally. The more he got, the cheaper the prices were getting; and the cheaper it was for him, the cheaper it was for his kingpins to sell it and so forth. The way J.R was feeling, I'm sure the loads would get even bigger. The competition was getting wiped out damn near completely, which was the result of them trying to break in the stash houses and trying to rob the runners if they couldn't make any money, then they were gonna try to take it. It was like that in every city, but none of the kingpins wanted to tell Beezy because he would let J.R know. They didn't want J.R to get upset. They wanted to keep everything smooth with him, so the retaliation game was strong. Anybody that tried them in any way was fucked up bad or killed. They had to stand on their principal to keep their name strong, and of course, J.R and Umbrella's names was strong. Any crew that was suspected in any way coming at them or trying to rob them had the execution team come through and spread bullets everywhere. The murder game and rate was at an all-time high, but this was part of business.

But seven thousand miles away in Japan, J.R. was very comfortable. There were no worries in his $800-a-night hotel, getting a full body massage from two Japanese women with his mind on expanding more as well as Tianna but also Yasmine. He felt kinda bad about that, but it was the truth. But J.R was human, and we can't help what we want. After his massage, he tipped both women a hundred dollars each and went to relax in the hot tub with a huge TV screen facing him. He turned it on and sipped on some expensive wine complimentary from the hotel. He then called Ron Ron, but he didn't answer. Seconds later, he called J.R right back. "Yo wassup, my boy. How is Japan treating you?"

J.R replied, "Everything is lovely, fam, business as usual. I got a few meetings in the morning and have to handle some business for Billy. I'll most likely cut myself into the deal as well, you know?"

Ron Ron replied, "Damn right! If it don't make money, it don't make sense, you feel me?"

J.R then said, "Real shit! But yo, how is everything on your end? How is the money flowing?"

"Everything is beautiful. I'm just building, and I don't plan to stop until we own everything one day!"

J.R smiled and said, "That's the ultimate plan. But cool. How is the fam? How is the wedding planning going?"

"It's going great, and thanks for paying for everything."

J.R replied, "Shit, your rich ass can afford it, but I just wanted to do it, anyway. And trust me, I will be front and center on y'all day."

Ron Ron said, "I hope so since you are my best man and my daughter's godfather."

They both laughed and J.R said, "True, true." They talked a little longer, then they hung up. J.R then texted Tianna and told her good morning because it was now morning in the States.

She replied, "Hey, baby. Thanks for the gifts."

He replied, "What gifts? Wrong person." He sent with a *lol* at the end."

She then replied, "Don't play with me. You know you the only person I want."

He then replied, "Yeah, I know. You're welcome, baby. All I wanna do is make you happy, and I promise when I get back we are going on a vacation so we can catch up and spend time."

She then said, "I can't wait. I really miss you."

He then said, "Likewise, baby, likewise." He sent a heart and a kiss.

J.R had a busy day in the morning. There was a lot of work to do with Yasmine and Billy's lawyer, so he then dried off from the hot tub and went to sleep.

Beezy was still excited about the news J.R gave him. That morning, his driver came to pick him up in his black Bentley with Revell in the passenger seat with a big 44 on his side and an AK-47 in the trunk. Beezy had stops to make and kingpins to check on everywhere. He would collect money from the day before and give solutions to any problems anybody had. But first, he told the driver to take him to Youngs Park. He had to go holla at his youngins about the meeting with the record label and, of course, the contracts Stacey faxed him that morning. When he pulled up, he seen them already out and moving that work early. The Bentley pulled up on them, and they already knew it was Beezy. Nobody else in the city had a brand-new top-of-the-line Bentley like that. The window rolled down and Beezy said, "What up? Y'all get in."

They said, "For real?"

"He said, "Yeah, get in."

At first, they were a little worried because Beezy never invited them in his car before, but they got in anyway and quickly asked, "Is everything okay, LB? We gave the money from yesterday's pack to Li'l Ray," who was Beezy's underboss.

Beezy smiled and said, "Nah, everything is cool. I'm not here for that." He then pulled out the contracts and asked, "Y'all still trying to make moves in the music game?"

They quickly said, "Damn right!" He then broke it down to them that he had a meeting for them the next day with Cold Cash

Records, which had a partnership with a major label and the biggest machine in the business.

They immediately got excited and said, "Real shit?"

Beezy said, "Yeah, I got y'all, but first, I need y'all to sign with my management company and we can go from there." They didn't hesitate. One minute later, they were officially the first group of artists on Umbrella Music Management, and Beezy felt proud of himself. He never saw these types of moves in his future. Everything was going great, and he planned to keep expanding. He then asked them, "What's y'all group name?"

They said, "Youngs Park Boys."

Beezy sat for a second and said,'" Nah, that's too much. You gotta be more simple with it, and since y'all two of my best corner boys, how about y'all call y'all selves Corner Boyz AKA C-Boyz?"

They said, "Yeah, we wit it." They were just excited to be getting this deal. They dapped up Beezy and got out of the car and went back to the block.

Beezy rolled down the window and said, "What are y'all doing?"

They then replied, "Going back to finish getting these packs off for you."

Beezy laughed and said, "Nah, y'all bout to be stars. No more packs for y'all. I need to make sure my artists take no prison chances. Li'l Ray gonna come get that work from you. Y'all retired. Don't touch no more."

They said, "Bet!"

Beezy said, "Answer your phone later. I got somebody coming to pick y'all up and take y'all shopping for the rest of the day. I need y'all in the best shit and plenty jewelry. Everything is on me, my treat. You gotta look that look when you sign that contract and jump in that rap game. Your image sells more records than your music."

They said, "Bet."

Beezy's driver pulled off, and he went to handle biz for the rest of the day.

Li'l Pat was still pissed off because he didn't know who sent those li'l niggas to try to rob one of his stash houses. He was rolling through Prentis Park in his Range Rover when his phone rung. It was his lieutenant. He told him one of the dudes they had tied up in the spot was starting to talk. He couldn't take the torture no more. By this point, they had cut them up everywhere with razor blades and pouring salt in the cuts. Whoever he was keeping quiet for wasn't worth it anymore. Li'l Pat said, "I'ma talk to him myself." When he pulled up everybody started running up to his truck trying to dap him up, showing love. Pat had a lot of respect in the city. He went inside the spot and saw how fucked up the dudes were. He told both of 'em, "Look, do you want your life, or are you gonna keep playing games?"

Thirsty, hungry, tired, weak, could barely see, beat badly, and cut up, one said something real low and could barely get it out, "Sttttt...Stt...Steve...Steve."

Li'l Pat said, "Who is Steve?"

The young boy didn't respond. I think at this point he took his last breath. Pat yelled, "Fuuuuckkk!" He then thought maybe Steve was an enemy of J.R, and even though he said he wasn't gonna tell J.R about this, he was thinking maybe he should just in case this situation was deeper than he thought. Since J.R was out the country, he had to call Beezy. Beezy's phone started ringing back to back. He finally answered, "Yo, wattup."

Li'l Pat was like, "Yo, we got a problem."

Beezy responded, "What is it?"

Li'l Pat said, "Some li'l niggas tried to rob one of the stash houses, and we got a name out of 'em of who sent them, but we don't know who the fuck he is. It's some nigga named Steve."

Beezy then said loudly, "Steve?"

The second he said Steve, Revell reacted and said, "I know exactly who that is."

Beezy said, "Oh yeah?"

Revell said, "Yeah, J.R wants that nigga dead. I know exactly where he lives."

Beezy said, "Bet, let's go see him." Before they could even get to the house, Revell spotted Steve in the passenger seat of a Honda Accord about two blocks from his crib. He told the driver to turn around, and he bussed a U turn in the middle of the street fast. Steve wasn't aware who it was, so he just sat there in the car as the person driving the car was walking back to the car. But Beezy's Bentley pulled in front of the Honda, blocking it in with Revell hopping out immediately. The second Steve saw Revell, he started scrambling. See the streets talk, and when Steve got out of jail, I'm sure he found out J.R was looking for him and that Revell was down with J.R now. He knew Revell put that murder game down with no problem. He tried to scramble out of the car and run, but it was too late. Revell had already put a hot bullet in his neck. He hit the ground instantly. Revell walked up to him and said, "I got good news and bad news."

Steve lay there, looking at him really bloody and hurt.

Revell said, "The good news is, J.R is happy that he got the money you owed him, but the bad news is, he told me to take you out." And *bam*, Revell put three bullets in his head, leaving his brain scattered all over the sidewalk. Beezy was watching this, and it made him realize how powerful J.R was. How could he be thousands of miles away and making things happen and he didn't even know it was happening? Beezy used to look up to his uncle Rick a whole lot, but to see the power, the money, the respect, and fear people had for J.R, and the way he handled business made him look up to and admire J.R even more. He was only four years older than him. Revell and Beezy then texted J.R with "Took care of Steve," but J.R was asleep. This was the middle of the night in Japan.

EPISODE 26

Falling for a New Love

Speaking of Japan, Yasmine couldn't sleep. She tossed and turned, thinking about how she was attracted to J.R and wanted him. She could still smell his cologne from lunch earlier. She had never met anyone like him, and she was interested and could not wait to see him again in the morning. As she lay in her XXL king-size bed, in her 2.7-million-dollar home, she had plenty of money, a high rank in her company, and a very bright future, with no one to share it with. Trust me, she has options, but no one could sweep her off her feet until now. J.R did, and he didn't even really try. There was just something about him that she continued to think about him until she finally fell asleep.

J.R woke up with his phone ringing. It was Billy. "How did everything go yesterday?"

"Perfect," he responded. "We're almost at a number and terms we all can agree on."

J.R replied, "Great, great. Well, that means maybe we won't have to be down here the entire month as planned. If we wrap that up, we can then fly back to the States." That was kind of a relief to J.R. He did miss Tianna, his li'l sister, and the rest of his people. He wanted to check on Deja and her baby girl and make sure his streets and money were flowing right. He also needed to see Ron Ron and Stacey to check on everything else, but in the back of his mind, he still was lusting after Yasmine. But after he and Billy hung up, he showered, got dressed, and waited for his car to pick him up.

When he arrived, he spotted Yasmine, sitting really pretty at the head of the table in the meeting. She took her finger and directed him to come over to her with a grin on her face like a high school girl. She had a big crush on him. As he came and sat beside her, she whispered to him, "How was your night?"

He said, "Awesome, I can't complain."

He then asked her the same, and she responded, "Not so good."

J.R then looked concerned and asked, "Why, what's wrong?"

But he wasn't prepared for what she was about to say. Her exact words were, "It would have been better if I felt your dick going in and out of me all night."

J.R got hard as a rock instantly; the lust on his face for her was very noticeable, and she could see that he wanted her to. Throughout the meeting, they texted each other constantly. J.R wasn't worried about paying attention in the meeting because Billy's lawyer was handling everything. They went back and forth for three hours until the meeting was adjourned. Her pussy was so wet that she started to get uncomfortable among everyone. They then texted "Meet me downstairs."

J.R told Billy's lawyer that they were once again going to lunch to talk more of the deal. Billy's lawyer looked at J.R like, "Huh? Were you paying attention? We closed the deal in the meeting. It was $325 million. Billy bought 35 percent of the company, and you own several shares and stocks in the company, as well as a gift from Billy."

J.R didn't know the exact worth of the shares, but he knew it had to be good. J.R said, "Great, but, um, let Billy know I will call him soon." They left immediately as her car picked them up. They went at each other, kissing uncontrollably. She didn't live far away, so when the driver pulled up to her beautiful home, they stopped briefly just to get out and go inside. They kissed nonstop, going up her steps and ripping each other's clothes off. When they made it to her bed, J.R put on a condom and dove right in, hitting that phat, juicy, wet pussy, slow, fast, then hitting her from the side, holding her big pretty breasts as they kissed; and she moaned, cumming all over his dick back to back. She never had dick this good ever. They were switching positions constantly, and this pussy was so good to J.R

STREET WEALTHY

that he felt the condom break but he didn't care. As she was riding him, she looked in his eyes, and she realized her feelings went from lust to now really feeling J.R, she didn't want this moment to end. He turned her around, pounding the shit out of her from the back as he wrapped his arm around her neck in a choking way, and she was loving it. J.R was so into this pussy that he even shot the club up, sending a whole week worth of backed-up nut deep in her. They both fell breathing hard, feeling really relaxed and satisfied. They lay there naked until they fell asleep.

When they woke up a few hours later, it was around 4:00 p.m. Tianna, Billy, and Ron Ron had all left missed calls on his phone. He lay there thinking like, That shit was mind-blowing. Speaking of blowing, she had gone down and was sucking him so good that he couldn't move. Her head game was top notch. Not quite as good as Tianna's, but it was close. They fucked about four more times after that. At this point, it was now dark outside, and J.R needed to contact Billy. He called, and Billy answered, "Yo, J.R, you good?"

J.R then replied, "Yeah, after lunch I was really tired. I ended up going back to the hotel and fell asleep."

Billy said, "Cool, the deal is done, so it's all good and I handled everything else. So we flying back in my jet in the a.m. to the States."

J.R said, "Cool." And they hung up.

Yasmine had a look on her face like, *Damn, now you're going to leave me.* Then she asked, "How long will you be in Japan?"

J.R replied, "Well, the private jet is taking us back in the morning." She then got sad and put her head down. J.R kissed her cheek and said, "Everything is going to be okay."

She then said, "When will I see you again?"

J.R said, "Soon, very soon. I promise." That made her feel much better. She never did this before. She wasn't that type of girl, but she couldn't control herself. And just like that, she caught feelings for J.R. He made love to her over and over that night. When the sun came up, she was asleep. He kissed her on her lips and slid out without waking her. J.R had no time to even shower. He had to get to his hotel and grab his things before Billy's jet left for the States. After about six and a half hours, the kingpin of all kingpins was back home.

79

EPISODE 27

Back from Japan and to Reality

J.R told no one he was home early. He went to see his bud connect. He hadn't touched bases in a while, but that was usually how
they did business. The person, or should I say people, because
it was a few of them that worked together that supplied thousands
of pounds weekly to certain people; and J.R was one of them. They
were at one of their car dealerships located in Chesapeake. J.R pulled
up in his Porsche 918 Spyder, rolling dolo, with no shooter, just his
P-416 automatic weapon on his back seat. They were just getting
out of a meeting with their salesmen, and J.R walked in, looking
like he was rich enough to buy the whole car lot. One of 'em quickly
said, "Wattup, J.R? Damn, my nigga, you definitely coming up faster
and faster. Every time I see you, your cars get more exotic, and your
clothes get harder to pronounce." They all laughed.

J.R smiled and said, "Hey, you already know I stay about my
business, but what's good though? Y'all got a minute to talk?"

Another one of them said, "Do we? Anybody that spends
$500,000 with us a week, I got time for anything."

J.R said, "Bet. Look, I know y'all pretty strong, and I love this
extra bread I have been making with y'all. We had an agreement. It
was lovely, but like all things, renegotiations often happen. And with
that being said, I just came from Asia, and I met a lot of people, one
of which is extremely heavy with the bud and I'm talking grade A
plus gas!"

80

One of them said, "Damn, J.R, so you're saying you done doing business with us?"

J.R responded, "See, that's why you have one mouth and two ears. You need to listen more and talk less. I wasn't finished. You know expanding is what I do. I'm addicted to growth. I can't get comfortable at one level too long, so going up is always necessary. And what I learned in Japan recently is that all lucrative businesses do not have to be started from the ground up. You can take a company, reconstruct it, and make your profits ten times the original. So I'm saying that to say this, instead of y'all supplying me, let's change the narrative a bit. Let's say I could hit y'all with twice the amount. You get a better quality at half of what you pay. What would you say to that?"

One responded, "I would say you are full of it and playing."

J.R responded really calmly, "Have I ever been the type to play?"

One responded, "Nah, not at all. Hey, I'm with it, especially if my lifestyle starts to look like yours, because you are definitely eating!" The other two agreed as well. J.R shook hands with them and invited them to come party with him in a few days to celebrate. See, the one thing about J.R that separated him from others was taking anything he learned in life and applying it to what he was doing. Think about it, he was taking $500K a week and spending it with them; he would then take the product he got from them and make max profit from $2.5 to $4 million, and that was cool but now he upgraded to a bigger connect and reconstructed their situation by getting them a better product for half the price, which would make their customers happier and also make their profits go up. Instead of him making $2 to $4 million a week, he was probably gonna make four times that with just them alone, and plenty more outside of them. This is exactly what he learned in Japan. J.R's business smarts was increasing rapidly with a combination of his power. He was becoming damn near invincible.

Sealing the Deal

Meanwhile, at LaGuardia Airport in Queens, New York, Beezy and the C-Boyz had just landed. They were headed to Manhattan to Cold Cash offices to talk with Steph. He was excited about the opportunity but also had a little anxiety about the situation, not knowing if they would get signed or not. When they arrived, Steph's assistant guided them to the conference room. When they walked in, Steph and two reps from the major label were present, smiling, and everyone shook hands. Beezy got straight to it. He exaggerated the group a li'l bit by saying they were already doing big numbers in Virginia. I'm sure the very expensive jewelry they were wearing might have made it seem real, and the fact that the labels did love the music they heard was good but the image made it even better. The labels felt that they didn't need the artists' development. They were saving a lot of money from the start. Long story short, they offered them a pretty good deal—a three-million-dollar signing bonus, and they wanted to start working immediately. They wanted the C-Boyz to be the next breakout group. They were prepared to put a lot of money behind them for marketing and budget. It was a deal; Beezy made his Instagram story a video of them signing their contracts with Cold Cash and Max Pay Records. The Corner Boyz was now official. Beezy wanted them in the studio ASAP, so he called Ron Ron to let him know he needed a state-of-the-art recording studio with a big office in it. Ron Ron told him, "No problem." It would be available in a week or two, and that was that. They flew back to the 757 right after the meeting. It was time to build.

J.R really didn't have any plans to meet with anyone that first day back, other than surprising Tianna later that night. Ron Ron was in California doing business. He just bought about two hundred acres of land and was developing a legal weed farm and compound. It was a billion-dollar business, so of course you know J.R wanted in. He texted Beezy, only to stop and holla at 'em briefly to spread a message to the other kingpins later that day, but Beezy didn't see the message. He had his phone on airplane mode while he was on his flight and forgot to turn it back. Since he didn't respond, J.R stopped by his spot. He was close by, anyway. When he pulled up, all his cars were there, so J.R figured he must be home, not knowing he went to New York that morning so he wasn't driving anything. Either way, Beezy was back in Virginia, and an uber was bringing him to the crib. He didn't even call his driver. He always felt safe in Norfolk. J.R rang the doorbell twice. No one came, so he turned to walk back to his car. Beezy's door opened, but it was Porsha that opened it to say, "J.R, hey, how are you?"

J.R looked like, "Um, okay. Hey, stranger, it's been a while. How is business? Is Ron Ron getting you right?"

She said, "Yes, everything is perfect."

J.R said, "Cool, I stopped to holla at LB and let him know I'm back in the states. I'm busy tonight, so I need him to spread some words throughout the camp for me." Porsha, thinking it would be a few hours before Beezy got home, told J.R she would let him know; but it would be a while, not knowing he was on his way to the house. So J.R said, "Cool, I will just call him later. I'ma just get Revell to spread the word for me."

Before he could finish his sentence, she cut him off saying, "Oh no, come in. I will get in contact with him real quick. Just come in for a second."

J.R looked hesitant but said, "Mmmmm...okay, cool."

She dialed Beezy twice, only getting his answering machine. "You reached LB. Leave a name and number. I will hit you back."

She said, "Damn, I can't reach him either."

J.R said, "Cool, talk to you later."

But she cut him off again, saying, "Hold on, I have a duffel of money for Ron Ron from a bunch of salons. I didn't really want to keep sitting on until he got back. Since it's your money anyway, I might as well give it to you now."

J.R kinda smirked and said, "True I guess you're right."

She went in her closet to get it, came back, and handed it to J.R. He didn't even look in it. He just tried to get out of there. But she boldly grabbed his hand and pulled him close to her and kissed him. He jerked back as fast as he could with her pecking the side of his mouth. He quickly said, "Yoooo, Porsha, what was that?"

She immediately looked embarrassed and said, "J.R, I'm sorry. I don't know what got over me."

He was like, "No, we can't do that. We can't take it there. LB is my boy."

She repeatedly said, "Sorry." She was looking nervous and embarrassed, but the truth was, the day J.R put her in a position to run those shops and be successful, she started building a crush on him. She never came at him like that before because they barely saw each other plus she knew it was a messy situation. But at this moment, she just went for it, thinking he would be with it. Even though he rejected her, the fact that he was loyal to Beezy made her like him even more. At that very split second, the door unlocked and opened. It was Beezy. He came in, looking really confused.

J.R quickly said, "B, wassup?"

And Porsha said, "Hey, bae, how was your flight?" She ran and hugged him. "J.R has been trying to reach you but couldn't, so he stopped by and I had this money to give him." Beezy looked down and saw the duffel bag on the floor. He also looked at his phone, realizing that it was still on airplane mode and none of his calls or messages could come through, so that quick feeling of "What the fuck is going on here?" calmed down a little.

J.R changed the mood up real quick and told him, "Look, I'm back, but I still need you in charge for a couple more days. I promised Tianna we would spend time."

Beezy said, "Okay, bet." But it was in a low-pitch, kinda-suspicious tone. He dapped him up, grabbed the duffel, and bounced. As he left out the door, Beezy saw Porsha's eyes follow J.R, and eyes don't lie. Even though he didn't say anything, he knew right then and there that Porsha wanted J.R.

EPISODE 29

Business Before Emotion

The next morning, J.R woke up feeling a little woozy from the night before and a bit dehydrated from lots of expensive wines, liquors, and champagne. He couldn't help but smell the aroma of breakfast cooking and a fine woman walking up to the bed, kissing him and saying, "Good morning, baby. How are you feeling?"

J.R then said, "I'm good, bae." But really, his head was pounding. But Tianna was looking so good. He just ignored the headache he was feeling and told her, "Baby, you look absolutely radiant." She smiled so hard and looked back at him, kissing him again then going back downstairs to finish breakfast. She was geeked up. They were spending time and he put her over his operation. They had an amazing date the night before, taking a helicopter to Atlanta just to have dinner at the Bones Restaurant and place after place to follow that, enjoying each other until they made it back to Tianna's spot. They didn't even have sex. He just held her until they fell asleep. It made her love him even more.

While J.R was enjoying his morning with Tianna, Beezy was headed to the studio to see the progress the C-Boyz were making. Ron Ron's construction and developing team wasn't finished with the official Umbrella Music Studio, yet so they were renting out a spot in the beach, getting twelve-hour blocks at a time. When Beezy pulled up in his Mercedes truck, he grabbed his Glock 9 out of the console and texted Revell his address. J.R wanted all the shooters and underbosses to know where the kingpins and lieutenants were at all times just in case something popped off, especially if they were traveling alone. They also must keep a heavy handgun and an automatic weapon at all times. Beezy kept the Mac 11 with the extended clip in his Mercedes truck. Every car had something different. He then went into the studio. This banging-ass beat was playing. Tyon was in the booth, about to lay down a hook for the beat. Ravon was rolling up a backwoods with some stupid gas in it. The engineer was getting the beat levels right and sitting on the studio couch was two li'l bad hood janks they met the night before at the club. When they noticed Beezy, Ravon waved at the engineer and signaled for him to cut off the beat. Beezy said, "Wattup?"

Tyon came out of the booth and said, "What's good, LB?"

Beezy then replied, "Business as usual, just came to see what kind of progress y'all making with these records before I go make moves in the streets. The record label wants three to four good songs in the next couple of weeks, and they want to pick one to start building y'all brand Corner Boyz, and hopefully it'll be a hit."

They said, "Yeah, we were cooking up some good shit. Wait till we play what we did last night." He inhaled and exhaled the blunt, then passed it to Ravon.

Beezy said, "Yeah, play it." But as he was saying it, somebody entered the building. It was two detectives. Beezy walked up to the front quickly, hoping they wouldn't smell the weed that was back in the engineer room and closing the door.

One of the detectives said, "Just the person we were looking for."

Beezy looked at 'em with his face balled up and said, "Me? Nah, you must have me mistaken."

The detective said, "Brandon Powell Jr., right? Better known as Li'l Brandon or LB? Or Beezy right?"

Beezy said, "Yeah, that's me. I ain't did shit, so what you want with me? And how you know I was here?"

The detective then said, "We came to see you at your condo, but since we saw you in a rush to leave, we decided to follow you. And here we are." The detective said it while smiling.

Beezy said, "So wassup, what do you want?"

They then said, "Look, you can stop trying to hide the weed smell. We are homicide detectives. We don't give a damn about drugs, but we're here as a follow-up to your uncle, Rickey Powell. We just wanted to know if you knew if he had any enemies who wanted to see him dead."

Beezy said quickly, "Nah, I don't know nothing, and plus my uncle was a stand-up dude. Everybody had love for him and respected him."

The detective then said, "You sure about that?"

Beezy said, "Of course. I'm sure."

The detective then said, "Oooh, okay, cool, because I'm looking at an affidavit that has his name on it, speaking on a lot of people back in the day. You sure none of them might want revenge for his testimony?"

Beezy said, "What? My uncle did his time in '01 and completed his whole stretch. That's bullshit. He ain't snitch on nobody."

The detective grinned and said, "I wasn't talking about that time."

Beezy started looking confused.

The detective continued, "I'm talking back in the early '90s, when you were just a kid. He got raided in one of his crack houses and was charged with trafficking and distributing. He was looking at some heavy time, even more than he did later on."

Beezy was in disbelief as the detective pulled out a copy of the affidavit stating the names of the drug dealers his uncle testified on. None were familiar to Beezy except one. Brandon Powell Sr., that was Beezy's father, who had been locked up since Beezy was a kid. He never went to visit him. He felt that his father left him to grow up without him, but his uncle, his dad's brother, was there his whole life. He had much love for his uncle, but at this moment, he discovered that his uncle was the reason his father wasn't in his life all those years. He started to feel bad for not going to see him or not writing any letters back to him. Even as the high-level drug dealer, killer, and boss, Beezy was, at this very moment, filled with a bunch of mixed emotions. It started with the fact that he noticed how his lady

Porsha felt about J.R and now finding out his uncle that he loved and respected and thought so highly of was the reason he had no dad growing up because he set his dad up to go to prison. He then told the detectives, "Look, I don't know anything."

The detective said, "Well, if you find out anything, let us know." And they handed him a card then left. Beezy went back in the studio session as the track they wanted him to hear was playing. Everybody was hyped, but Beezy was in a zone. He just rolled up some gas, sat back, and smoked to calm his nerves. He didn't say anything the whole session, just sat there quietly.

After a few hours passed, J.R texted Beezy and told him that he needed him to pick up some money in Suffolk then go out to downtown Newport News to holla at Big Andrew, which had two attempts of somebody trying to rob the drug and money stash houses in that area, as well as Denbigh. J.R was killing the competition, so a lot of crews were mad and hungry. J.R wanted any information on the robbery attempts, and he was gonna handle it from there. But at that moment, he and Tianna were continuing their day together, about to go shopping. J.R wanted Revell to roll with him so he could focus on Tianna and not have to watch his back, so Dre was gonna assist Beezy out Suffolk and Newport News. Beezy responded, "Bet." He then went and met up with Dre. A couple of hours later, they were leaving downtown Suffolk and heading to Newport News. Beezy and Dre were riding in silence, and mainly because Beezy had a lot on his mind. Dre didn't really like Beezy, because he felt that he should be in Beezy's spot as J.R's second in command. So much was running on both of their minds. Beezy couldn't stop thinking about his uncle and dad. Dre was feeling some type of way because of the hate in his heart for Beezy and also being mad at J.R, but one thing J.R told many of his people was, never make business decisions out of emotion because moving off impulse could hurt you in the long run. But in this case, it was immediately. Beezy kinda bucked on Dre like, "Yo, the fuck is your problem, nigga? I have been sensing a lot of negative energy from you."

Dre tapped on the driver's shoulder directing him to pull over and said to Beezy, "Who the fuck you think you talking to? Do I look like one of them li'l niggas from Norfolk that you control every day? Watch your muthafucking mouth when you talking to me."

Beezy put his hand on his Glock 9 the second Dre got his last word out and replied, "Do we have a problem? Let's handle it now."

Dre grabbed his Four Pound, turned around, and pointed it at Beezy. Beezy was pointing his at him as well. Dre told him straight up, "I did this shit only on the strength of J.R, but I don't fuck with newcomers like that. I don't answer to nobody. J.R might trust you, but I don't, my nigga."

Beezy, with a lot of aggression in his voice, returned words, saying, "Damn, my nigga, you a hater like that? You mad because J.R rock with a realer nigga more? Huh? You mad because me and him got tight because he recognized the hustler and businessman in me that he never saw in your emotional bitch ass? Huh?"

Dre was furious after that statement. He said, "Tight? You think J.R tight with you?" Not realizing he was letting his emotions get the best of him, he got deeper, saying, "If J.R was so tight with you, why would he get your uncle smoked?"

Even though that happened before J.R and Beezy became tight, Beezy got extremely pissed from that statement and said, "What the fuck did you say, nigga?"

Dre replied, "Yeah, I said it. J.R got your uncle hit, and I know for a fact, because I'm the one that pulled the trigger. Fuck all y'all outsiders. I'm a day 1. We don't need none of y'all for real."

Beezy, already having a bullet in the head of his Glock, squeezed immediately, but his gun jammed. Trying a second time got the same result. Dre then started squeezing his four pound while Beezy ducked low, and the bullets went straight to the back window, putting holes all in it and breaking it up. Beezy pushed the back door open, scrambling out fast as he could while Dre kept shooting and missing him every time; but that wasn't usual for Dre. He was a sharpshooter, but he was off balance at this moment. Once he realized he was out of bullets and Beezy had gotten away, he quickly grabbed his other gun out his pocket, put it to the driver's head, and told him, "Drive." He then realized what he had said. He knew childhood friend or not that J.R was gonna be pissed about what he just told Beezy. He knew

J.R long enough to know that it might not be safe for him to come around, so he told the driver to step on it. He needed to go lay low until he could figure out what to tell J.R about this.

Beezy immediately texted J.R like, "Yo, we gotta talk asap."

Dre called J.R. When he answered, he quickly said, "J.R, I fucked up. I let my emotions get the best of me."

J.R was walking through Lynnhaven Mall with Tianna at the time. He was looking real confused and said, "Dre, wtf are you talking about?"

Dre, real frantic and emotional, started saying, "I thought we was day ones. How you gonna put these outside niggas ahead of me? We played in the sandbox as babies. We know each other's family, them niggas only around to eat off you."

J.R then said, "Dre, where the fuck is all this coming from?"

Tianna then rubbed J.R's arm and said, "Bae, is everything okay?" J.R didn't respond to her.

Dre said, "Look, shit fucked up. That nigga Beezy and me just shot it out. I never liked that bitch-ass nigga, anyway."

J.R said, "What? Shot it out? The fuck is you talking about? Y'all not handling business or getting my fucking money?" J.R was pissed.

Dre said, "That nigga thought he could talk to me like one of them li'l niggas, so we exchanged words. He said what he said. My pride got the best of me, so I kinda told him how I put a whole clip in Rick's old ass. He tried to shoot at me, but his gun jammed. I squeezed back, but he slid out the whip. I was so mad that my aim was off and he ran off somewhere, and J.R, you know it ain't no coming back from shit like that. He probably out for me, so I got to smoke his ass if I see him first. I'm sure he probably out for you too."

J.R then got quiet, thinking, *See, this is the reason I didn't put Dre in a high position. He definitely is not built for business.* J.R calmed down and said, "okay, just meet me in Virginia Beach. I will take care of this situation. Just bring me my money. Everything's gonna get squared away."

Dre knew right then and there by J.R getting so suddenly calm that if he came to bring him that money, he would never walk away.

He would get killed instantly. Dre said, "Okay, give me thirty minutes. I'm on my way."

J.R hung up. Of course, Dre was lying. He looked at the $800 grand that was in the duffel bag he just picked up in Suffolk. He told the driver, "Pull over." He made him get out and drove off. He had to get out of there, heading straight to his baby momma's house to lay low and figure out his next move.

Beezy, after texting J.R, then called his underboss, Li'l Ray, to come pick him up. He was beyond angry when Ray got there. Beezy hopped in, not saying much. Li'l Ray looked concerned, trying to figure out what was going on and why Beezy was stranded in the middle of nowhere. He asked him, "LB, what's going on, bro?"

Beezy just said, "take me to my spot in Virginia Beach." And that's what he did. When he got there, Li'l Ray followed him inside. Beezy went straight to his kitchen bar and poured him a glass of Casa Dragones tequila. He drank it and poured another. Li'l Ray knew something wasn't right. Beezy then went to his bedroom and then to the bathroom. He turned on the shower and stayed there with the water running on him for a long while thinking about everything he found out all at once. It was like everything was going so perfect, now this. His emotions were out of control. He wanted to kill J.R for what he heard he did to his uncle, but at the same time, he was glad J.R killed his uncle for taking his dad away from him his whole life. He was stressed out at this point, so after he got out of the shower, he continued to drink, telling Li'l Ray, "I need you to handle business for the rest of the day."

He said, "Okay."

They dapped up, and he left. Beezy didn't know what was gonna happen next. He sat there, sipping and constantly pouring drinks. J.R texted him, "Where you at?" At first he wasn't sure if he should trust J.R because of what happened with him and Dre. He was sure Dre told him by now, and if J.R knew the cat was out of the bag about his uncle, then he probably would try and take Beezy out before he could get to him. He responded, "I'm at the beach spot. Come alone. Don't bring Revell or nobody, just me and you."

J.R pulled up within minutes. He figured that would be the spot Beezy was at. J.R was one of the few that knew about that spot. Not even Porsha knew he had that apartment. J.R did come alone, but he had his .357 Magnum revolver on him. He didn't know what was going through Beezy's head or if he believed Dre or not. The second Beezy opened the door, he and J.R looked at each other as if they were gonna fight or shoot it out. The moment was super tense. J.R said, "Yo, what the fuck is going on? Where is Dre?" J.R pretended he never spoke to Dre, but really, he had people out looking for him. Dre wouldn't last too much longer.

Beezy responded, "Fuck that nigga Dre. I don't know where the fuck he at, but yo, I need you to be straight up with me. Did you get my uncle hit? And if so, why?"

J.R gave this made up confused look and said, "What? The fuck is you talking about? Get your uncle hit? Why the fuck would I do that?"

Beezy responded, "Me and that hoe-ass nigga Dre shot it out. He obviously felt some way about me. He told me you put the order out on my uncle and he was the one that pulled the trigger."

For a second, J.R thought, *You know what, maybe I should just blues this nigga real quick to kill all this confusion.* But then he also thought about how bad this would hurt his business, so he said, "My nigga, what kind of sense do that make? You know I'm about business, and yeah I do put the murder game down if necessary, but what reason or why would it benefit me to kill him? You see how me and you do business at all levels. If anything, I would get money with your uncle, so tell me what would be the point?"

Beezy really couldn't answer that. He grabbed his drink and downed what was left in the glass and said, "You right. You right, my nigga. I'm tripping." But then he said, "So why would Dre say that?"

J.R responded, "Because Dre probably hates the fact that you came up in the camp so fast and higher than him. You know a nigga hating will do and say anything to get under your skin. Damn, my boy, you let that shit get to you? I thought you were stronger than that. We got millions of dollars on the table everywhere. Snap back in it, my boy, you losing it!"

Beezy grabbed the whole bottle of liquor and took a swig straight from the bottle. He really wanted to believe J.R because he started to look at him like a brother. He then said, "What about Dre though?"

J.R said, "Fuck Dre, anybody that put emotions over business and lie on my name like that gotta go ASAP!" He showed Beezy his phone and sent a text to Revell. "Take out Dre."

Beezy calmed down more, not knowing that Dre had a hit out on him already, and the beef between him and Beezy was settled. Dre had a whole clip coming to him, and it was time to get back to the money.

EPISODE 30

Hiding Out

Deep out in the woods right outside the 7 Cities, Dre had a baby by a chick nobody knew about. He hid her for a few reasons. One being for situations like this when he might have to lay low for a while. Also, she wasn't the prettiest chick, and he was kinda ashamed of that. He always made sure she was good though and took care of his child. As his baby momma and son slept, Dre was up, rolling blunt after blunt. He took a bottle of Martell to the head, thinking about how he let shit spiral out of control like this. He knew there was no way J.R would let this go. Then to make things worse, he ran off with J.R's money, damn! It was enough to slide out of town and keep it moving. Traveling on the road was too risky. J.R had people in damn near every city from Hampton Roads up to Alexandria, so he had to catch a plane. He had his baby momma and people to get him a fake ID and everything so he couldn't be tracked on a flight or anything. Even though Dre was a 100 percent ruthless killer, he knew he was no match for J.R's power. The night turned into day, and Dre was up and at it. He left fifty thousand on the living room table for his child's mother and son. He didn't tell her that he was leaving. He planned to call when he was stable.

He already got rid of Beezy's car that he stole the day before, so he set up an uber ride to take him to Norfolk International. He just wanted to get far away from Virginia as possible. As he was riding, all types of things were going through his mind. He had to stay high just to cope with it all, but the closer he got to the airport, the more relief

95

he felt. The driver looked back and told him he had one more person to pick up along the way, but he still would be at his destination on time. Dre was looking real uncomfortable about that, but what could he do? He had no other choice. He had his Skully down low with a hoodie over it. He wanted to be disguised as much as possible. When the uber picked up the other passenger, Dre kept looking at them out of the side of his eye, making sure it wasn't nobody J.R knew. He was paranoid as shit and needed another blunt. He had never been so nervous in his life. All he could think about was how many people he saw J.R ordered to be killed when they crossed him. Why would he be exempt? As they got to the airport, he thought maybe J.R would let it go because of their history, maybe because they grew up so tight, he would let this slide. But he should have known better because J.R moved off principle, and also if J.R let him slide, then other niggas would think it would be okay to cross him.

As Dre walked through the airport, he looked around to make sure nobody was following him. The only bag he had was the duffel, he quickly checked in and boarded the plane and took his seat, waiting impatiently for others to get seated and then takeoff. Even though he was actually getting away, his paranoia increased even more because he thought this was too good to be true. As time passed, the plane eventually took off. The estimated time would be around two and a half hours. His flight was headed to Miami. He knew J.R's old connect from back in the day lived out there, and Dre himself took many trips with J.R to score work. The plan was to take the money he took from J.R, get the old Miami connect to work out a deal for the cheapest price, and somehow get the work back to Virginia to people he knew that had nothing to do with Umbrella. He'd basically boss up and be the middleman between the Miami connect and some people back home.

When he finally arrived, it didn't take him very long to get in contact with him. He hit him up like, "Ernesto, what's good? This is Dre from Virginia. J.R's people, remember me?"

Ernesto replied, "Dre? Um yeah, yeah, how could I forget? What made you call me? It's been a while." Dre said, "Yeah, we had to slow down the operation when Steph got out of prison. He talked

J.R into investing money into the music business, thinking he was gonna be successful and leave the streets alone forever, but that didn't happen. So look, we back, and who better to do business with than my favorite Cuban?"

Ernesto said, "Oh yeah? I tell you what, meet me at my night club tonight around eleven. I should be free to talk at that point."

Dre said, "Okay, okay cool." As the day went on, Dre did a li'l shopping because he didn't bring any clothes with him and even tricked up a li'l money on this li'l bad jank he met at the mall. He thought in his mind that he could maybe get used to this Miami life-style. He'd make Ernesto think he was sending work to J.R and keep making money until he figured out something else. He'd network and grow, you know. But this was the plan for now. He got a hotel room and smashed that li'l bad chick he spent a couple racks on. He needed to kill time, anyway. They lay up, smoked a few blunts together, and fucked some more until it started getting late; and Dre basically dismissed her, sending her on her way. He took a shower and got fresh for the club. He even bought a li'l jewelry. He didn't want Ernesto to think nothing suspicious outside of what he told him. He even paid a few dudes he saw close by the club to go in with him to play the part. He needed it to look like J.R really sent him.

Dre and the random dudes were at the bar getting drinks when Ernesto came down from the upstairs part of the club. He recognized him instantly. He walked up, shaking his hand and saying, "Dre, long time no see. Come to my office. Let's talk."

Dre then told the other guys, "Wait there." As they walked through the crowd, Dre looked around at all the beautiful Cuban women that were dancing. Everything was going smooth, and his confidence had built back up. He thought it was over for him at first, but now he was feeling like maybe he could pull this off. They finally got to his office and sat down. Dre immediately put the duffel bag on his desk, getting straight to business, "Ernesto, I got 500 large for you, what can you do for that?"

Ernesto looked in the bag and said, "This is 500K?"

Dre, with a li'l smirk on his face, said, "Yeah, 500 bands. Let's do business."

Ernesto sat back and said, "Okay, okay I got you." He zipped the duffel bag up and handed it to his associate. He told Dre to follow his other associate to the back room to bag up the kilos. Dre then got happy, as he followed Ernesto's associate down the hallway. He knew it was on now, and he was further calculating in his mind the next move of his operation. But as he turned the corner, at this point going into the room, he glanced in and the first thing he saw was Revell sitting in a chair, holding a Beretta AR70/90. The loud club became to Dre's ears nothing but silence. All he saw was Revell mouth moving, saying, "J.R told me to give you this." He put bullet after bullet in him until Revell decided to stop shooting. His plan failed miserably. He had a better chance of staying out in the country with his baby momma because what Dre didn't know was, when he called Ernesto and gave him that story, Ernesto knew it was bogus because he and J.R had spoken recently when they came to open up the Umbrella Club in Miami. Since then they kept in touch. That's why he told him to come by the club later so he could call J.R, and this was how it ended for Dre.

Level Up

A few months passed. J.R and Beezy weren't beefing, but things weren't exactly perfect. Even though Beezy accepted what J.R told him, he still wasn't 100 percent sure of what really happened. He kinda kept one eye open with J.R. He did business with him, but he didn't trust him like before. That's also how he felt about Porsha. He still loved her, but he knew how she felt about J.R even though he never confronted her about it. He felt she would deny it, anyway. All in all, business was booming. The Corner Boyz had a single out that was getting a lot of attention. They were living in New York, working close with the label. It was important for building their brand, so they would have meetings with Beezy and sometimes J.R via FaceTime on the flat screen at the management office. They just shot a music video for their single two weeks prior out in Youngs Park that was soon to be released as well.

J.R and Tianna were getting stronger and stronger. He even asked her to live with him, but she kinda declined. She told him she wanted a ring first, and J.R respected that. He knew he wanted her in his life, so proposing was definitely a thought for him. Speaking of marriage, Ron Ron and Elmyra's big day was getting closer. Ron Ron's assistant, Shawn Floyd, was set to run the operations while Ron Ron went on his honeymoon.

J.R had been getting tons of texts from Yasmine, but he really didn't know how to respond. She wanted to build a relationship, and the truth was, he really did like her a lot. But he was in love with

Tianna. But instead of telling her that, he kinda led her on. Billy was super impressed by J.R bossing up. He definitely thanked Steph for connecting them in business and bought Steph a waterfront home in Virginia as his appreciation. J.R was now moving five times the work he was getting from the beginning. Money was pouring in so fast that it was getting harder to wash it even though Ron Ron was damn near building up the whole United States, it felt like, with business after business. Porsha also became a millionaire off the salons and shops. She started investing into a lot of other things as well.

Billy saw how J.R not only became extremely rich but also made everyone around him rich, and he admired that. So he had a proposition for J.R that could level him up even more. He invited J.R and all his Umbrella team to come join him at his club in Hampton. He wanted to celebrate their success. Everyone showed up; the night was full of laughs, drinking, dancing, and networking. Billy asked J.R to come to his office. When he got in there, he poured him a drink and asked him, "Are you satisfied?"

J.R looked around and said, "Nah, I'm not sure if I ever will be because as long as there are heights to get to, I'm reaching for it."

Billy said, "Right, right. So with that being said, I wanna offer you a proposition. I know I've been supplying you for a while now, and the supply is getting bigger and bigger. You make me a shitload of money, so I'm thinking, since what I supply you is probably more than everyone else I supply put together, then I don't need to deal with as many people as I do. I'm thinking I could sit you down with my connection and we could become partners. That way, we split the load from my connection, which would probably be twice as much as I'm getting now, and we pay him together. This way, you would be able to expand ten times as much." J.R, feeling a li'l tipsy, sat and thought for a second like, *Damn, this would be big.*

Truthfully, Billy was inching more and more into the corporate world, and with J.R being his partner, he knew he would have more time to buy, break down, and flip multibillion-dollar companies such as the one he got a piece of in Japan. He told J.R to think about it and let him know ASAP what his decision was, but J.R, being J.R, didn't need time to think. He was prepared to take things higher, and the sky was just the starting point. He accepted Billy's proposition, and he already mapped out in his mind how he was gonna handle everything. He was definitely gonna expand the amount of king-pins in Virginia. Instead of just the 757, now he would reach out to Richmond, Woodbridge, Alexandria, and etc. Although he already did business in those places by supplying people, he didn't have it structured like the 757 with kingpins and the chain of command. J.R then shook hands with Billy. "This calls for a toast," Billy said as they made their way back to the front area.

J.R went up to Beezy and told him he needed to promote his lieutenant up to kingpin if he was fit for it and his underboss up to lieutenant and so forth, because he was gonna be in charge of the whole 757 just like he was when J.R was in Japan. But now it would be a permanent position. J.R would then go up to Northern Virginia and build that up just like the 7 Cities. When that was on point, he would assign the same position he was giving Beezy up there. Beezy was excited even though there was still a li'l awkwardness between him and J.R, but business is business. So he dapped him up and went off to talk to his people about their promotion.

After everyone gathered around and they toasted to more and more success, the music came back on and the partying continued. Billy had it set up for all of J.R's kingpins to have their own separate VIP sections. Of course J.R had the biggest and best section with a lot of his friends and family. He had his active lieutenant, Beezy, and his underboss, Revell, as well as their ladies, Tianna, Tonya, and Porsha. Billy told J.R, "I invited many people from business ventures that I have going on around the world, and I want you to meet some of them."

J.R said, "Cool." But he sat with Tianna by his side looking extremely gorgeous in her Chanel pumps, Chanel dress, forty-thou-sand-dollar Birkin bag, and fifteen-thousand-dollar sew-in weave down to her ass with diamonds on her wrist, neck, and ears with per-fect makeup while sipping her martini. A group of people walked up to J.R's section, some appearing to be foreign—Asian to be exact and very wealthy. It was the CEO, reps, and guests of the big company Billy was partners with. J.R shook hands, meeting them for the first time, because while they were in Japan, J.R only met the president of the company, who was Yasmine. Speaking of Yasmine, Billy then said, "J.R, I'm sure you remember Yasmine Moon." She was also with them, and J.R didn't notice at first. Man, she was looking stunningly beautiful. J.R's whole mood changed, and his heart started beating fast as she walked toward him. First she was smiling, but then she noticed the pretty lady leaning on him, who was Tianna. Yasmine's face shifted fast, as she was gonna come hug him, but then she shook his hand. Billy then took his new business partners over to meet more people. Yasmine looked at J.R really pissed, but then turned her professional face back on.

Tianna then said, "Bae, she is really pretty."

J.R looked at her and said, "You think so?"

Tianna said, "Yes."

As she shook her head, J.R replied, "But, not as pretty as you, bae." And he kissed her on her forehead. J.R then said, "Excuse me, baby. I have to run to the bathroom."

She said, "Don't take long." She was winking her eye and grinning.

J.R walked through the crowd real swiftly and quietly grabbed Yasmine's arm, pulling her off to the side. He said, "How come you didn't tell me you were coming to the states?"

Looking really pissed and disappointed in him, Yanmine just said, "I wanted to surprise your ass, but I see I'm the one that got the surprise."

Looking and feeling emotional, J.R said, "Look, I can explain. I know I should have told you about her when I was in Japan, but what we shared, the moment, the momentum, and the connection, as well as the mood and the feeling were unreal and…and—"

Yasmine cut him off, saying, "And what? That's no excuse. We have been messaging, and talking on the phone for months. You didn't think to tell me something as important as that?"

J.R didn't know what to say. She pulled away from him, and then he grabbed her, saying." Look, Yasmine, I really care about you a lot. I know what the situation is, but I never wanted to hurt you. I think about you daily. You weren't just a thing. You mean a lot to me. How can we fix this?"

She said, "There's nothing to fix. You have a woman, so I guess that puts me back to being available for someone who is single and wants only me."

J.R responded, "I do want you. You have no idea what I go through between you and her."

Yasmine then said, "Well, you have to make a choice, and I'm not gonna wait forever." As she pulled away again, she was quietly saying before she walked away, "Oh and by the way, I'm three months pregnant." She blew a sarcastic kiss and walked away to catch back up with Billy, the CEO, and reps.

Surprises

Right at the very moment, J.R was about to level up and make the biggest move ever. Yasmine dropped this bomb on him, but he wouldn't let his emotions affect his business judgements. Billy introduced him to the connect, and he and J.R officially became partners. And if you thought money was pouring in before, then let's just say that wasn't even a third of what J.R was making now. Everyone was happy. They started seeing upgrades on every person in the camp lifestyle. More houses were built, more kids were spoiled, and more babies were made. Life was great for the Umbrella team, but the streets were extremely dangerous, now all throughout 757. With the way J.R took over Northern Virginia, the streets up there were just as bad, but like I said before, none of that affected J.R. He was back and forth from the States to Japan. One night he was in bed, holding Tianna and telling her there was no one else for him but her, and the next night, he was rubbing Yasmine's stomach while he held her in bed, kissing her neck and telling her he only had eyes for her. I guess that was easy to do when you had a twenty-million-dollar luxury private jet, and thirty thousand dollars for fuel was no money for J.R.

Over a course of months, about four to be exact, Ron Ron and Elmyra got married. Their wedding was nothing less than beautiful. All the guests were given diamond Rolex watches as a gift. This was J.R's idea. Ruth Chris catered, and the food was amazing. Elmyra was extremely beautiful, and Ron Ron looked happier than ever before.

To add on to paying for this gorgeous wedding, J.R sent them to Dubai for their honeymoon, and they returned to a 9.7-million-dollar mansion he had built from the bottom up. J.R had become like Billy in some ways. He bought nice things for his top earners, and Ron Ron made J.R a shitload of money.

The Corner Boyz were booming out of control with over five hundred million streams on their single. Their mixtape was the biggest project out. Their album did top numbers in the US and several other countries. Show dates were lined up for months. Beezy couldn't have been happier, but the C-Boyz weren't the happiest. I mean yeah, they both had nice foreign cars, nice jewelry, and a few bands in the stash; but the money wasn't coming like they thought it would. I mean, it seemed like everybody was eating good off them, and they were getting pennies. The label already had them recording a second project with an international tour set up to last eighteen months, but they felt they weren't even paid for everything else yet. They took a few days off to get their mind right and flew home to the 757. They stopped by the management office where Beezy happened to be that day. He spent more time there than ever before, mainly because he was signing more and more artists, and he felt he needed to be more hands on with them. Ravon and Tyon came into the building looking like rock stars. They had super expensive clothes, diamond teeth, necklaces, and their feet were drippy; but their attitudes were a li'l more cocky. They usually approached Beezy with lots of respect and fear, but on this day, it was different.

"Yo, LB, what the fuck, man? What's going on? We got one of the biggest singles in the world, with hundreds of millions of streams, mixtapes sales, six million albums sold, and Corner Boyz merchandise. And our mommas are still living out Youngs Park!" Ravon said with lots of anger in his voice.

Beezy reacted immediately while his underboss stood up, clutching his four pound. Beezy said with three times the anger and no hesitation, "Hold up, who the fuck you li'l niggas think you talking to? Y'all let that music shit get too far up y'all asses. Y'all do remember who the fuck I am, don't you? I will make you disappear before you blink twice. Them crackers up in that record label boosting y'all head up too fucken much."

As he pulled out his Glock 9, Tyon said, "Whoa, whoa, our bad, LB. We just frustrated. We thought with all the success, we would have made more money."

Beezy replied, "Look, li'l niggas. The music game is just like the dope game, it ain't no different. The same way y'all pumped pack after pack on them corners and made only a few grand a week, it's the same in the music business. You're just a worker for that label. They pay for everything. They make sure you want for nothing, but when the sales come in, they recoup every penny they spent. The bonus, the studio time, the beats, the videos, food, clothes, and expenses. All those ounces of weed y'all smoke ain't free. Every night you go to five-star hotels and have shopping sprees in every city, etc., etc. Plus they get first dibs on the profit, and then the manager gets paid, that's me. Then your lawyer, and you can't forget about Uncle Sam. And the little that's left is then yours. That Lamborghini that's parked outside, that could have been a house for your mom. You can't live my lifestyle in the music business. Those rappers y'all look up to are not rich like you think. Most of that shit is cap, and just like y'all, most of their shit is fronted by the record company, and they are living paycheck to paycheck. That's why y'all li'l niggas gotta be smart with your money. Get your mom a crib first, invest some bread, and stack up. Use the major label to build your brand, then go independent and keep most of the money."

They responded, "LB, you right, we were caught up in the hype."

Beezy responded, "I know damn well y'all are, but look, I'ma look out for your mom. I'ma get her a nice house in Virginia Beach only because I got love for y'all. But for now on, get your head in the game and off that fame shit. And I repeat, don't ever in your life come at me like that again. Trust me, it won't be pretty." He then sat his Glock on his desk.

They quickly said, "We're sorry, Beezy. It won't happen again."

He then said, "Yeah, get out of my office." And that was that.

EPISODE 33

Boss Power

As the due date for Yasmine to have the baby was getting closer, J.R thought it would be best for her to move to the States, but Yasmine was concerned about her career. As she told J.R, of course he was baffled and laughing uncontrollably. J.R said, "Career? Baby, why be the president of a company working for someone else when you can own several companies and be a CEO? I mean, being my lady, you never have to work another day ever and have anything you desire, but if you want to work, then figure out what it is you want to do and I got you, no limits!"

Yasmine had the biggest Kool-Aid smile while J.R kissed her stomach as they lay in bed. "So don't worry. You can put in your resignation ASAP, and I'm gonna build us a house in Los Angeles. And anything else you want, just name it." Yasmine felt so lucky. Other than the fact that she knew J.R was still with Tianna, she kinda felt deep inside that she was settling; but she was in love with him and they were about to have a child together and he spoiled her so much that she was addicted to it. The only problem was, she knew about Tianna, but she knew Tianna knew nothing about her. So she felt Tianna was more special to J.R, and it made her feel a kind of way. But she always shrugged it off.

Quantico FBI was getting fed up with the Virginia drug and violence activity, but with the way things were going, they couldn't figure out the source of the problem. They knew drugs were the cause, but with the way J.R had it structured, the feds had nothing to go on other than a few people here and there that they busted. They kicked in some stash houses and grabbed a few runners and corner boys and sent up the road, but no one would talk. J.R was feared so deeply that they would rather take a life sentence before giving him up, and with that being said, J.R wasn't even close on the FBI radar. Not yet at least. Their suspects were the Italians and old drug dealers that did years in prison, got out, and were thought to be moving low-key; but none of them ever had an operation like this or even close. So it would take a miracle for them to stop J.R. He was too many steps ahead of them.

Untouchable—untouchable was the word to describe J.R at this point. He was untouchable from his enemies and untouchable from law enforcement. He was not only protected by his own people but also by Billy's people and the connects' people. J.R was very valuable to a lot of people around the world. He was not just limited to Virginia anymore, even though that was where he was the kingpin of all kingpins and ran it as such. He was strong damn near everywhere else, supplying many different cities in other states as well as his legitimate businesses. No one would ever think a young black man that came from nothing would have this type of power, and as the months went by, the power grew, just like a ball rolling fast down a hill. J.R and Yasmine went on to have a healthy baby boy who wouldn't ever know what it feels like to struggle. J.R made sure he was gonna be good no matter what happened, as well as his mother. And yes, J.R proposed to Tianna. By this point, Yasmine accepted everything she felt. As long as she didn't have to see it, it was okay, and she didn't care because they were three thousand miles apart. She was in a very comfortable estate out in the LA hills, and Tianna had a very nice mansion built from the bottom up in Virginia right outside of Maryland. J.R couldn't let either of them go. He was in love with them both and had the money to take care of them both and gave them very nice lifestyles.

From Virginia to LA, LA to Virginia, in between, and beyond was J.R's constant travel route in private jets; and he was chauffeured around in the most expensive cars with three shooters at all times. Revell was now in charge of J.R's hit unit, mainly to take out out-oftowners that J.R supplied that either didn't pay what they owed or were facing fed time. J.R didn't take no chance of them cooperating with the authorities. See, in Virginia, most people knew better, but in different states, they might try J.R, especially if they didn't know his reputation well; but he always made sure he made examples out of them so the next person in that town knew better.

Boss Power 2

E arly one Friday morning, J.R had his usual meeting, but now it was a li'l different. Instead of meeting with the kingpins like he used to, the circle was much smaller. Now it was only Beezy, Ron Ron, Stacey, and Tequan from Manassas Park. He was in charge of all the kingpins in Northern Virginia, and of course, Beezy ran the 757. He discussed whatever business with them, and they would then have their own meeting later that day with the kingpins. Early in the meeting, Ron Ron and Stacey stressed to J.R that so much money was coming in that it was getting too hard to wash it all. J.R sat there looking kinda concerned, but then he calmly said, "Fix it, Stacey. That's why I pay you millions of dollars a year to fix problems, right?" Looking very serious, he also said, "If you can't, I will find someone who can. I'm too busy to do your job, so figure it out."

Stacey immediately replied, "Okay, I'm on it." He then told Beezy and Tequan, "Make sure all your kingpins switch up the stash houses every month. You gotta stay ahead of the competition and police. And every spot now gotta have a shooter at every door all day. I don't care if you have to do it in twelve-hour shifts, just keep my money protected. I'm not tolerating no more fuck shit because if I find out money's being stolen, it's a problem."

They both said, "I got it."

J.R then said, "That's it for today. Everybody can leave, but Ron Ron, you stay back for a second."

They all left except for Ron Ron. J.R asked, "How is marriage treating you?"

Ron Ron replied, "Great, everything is perfect."

"Okay, but look, I'm not sure if you're aware, but Stacey informed me there's a chick from Miami, Amelia Smith. She's been emailing every business your name is tied to, trying to contact you. She says she is six months pregnant."

Ron Ron loosened up his tie and poured a drink of the very expensive cognac J.R had on the round table then replied, "Yeah, I been trying to avoid her." He was looking a little stressed he sat for a second then said, "J.R, I fucked up. She's threatening to contact my wife. I don't need this right now. We're in a great space."

J.R also poured a drink and said, "Ron, listen, you can't let this get in the way of your happiness. We are in a position to handle things like this. You have to use your power in a situation like this, so how do you want to handle it?"

Ron Ron looking stressed out taking a sip of his drink and said, "J.R, I have no clue."

J.R then replied, "Don't worry. I will take care of this." Ron Ron's eyes got really wide. J.R started laughing and said, "No, not like that." Ron Ron looked relieved. J.R went on to say, "I know she lives in Miami, but I'm gonna put her in a nice condo in Tampa. That way, when your wife is in Miami with you, she will be far away. I will give her a nice allowance every month, let's say, um, $50,000. I'll make sure she or the baby want for nothing, plus I'll have her sign an agreement to keep her mouth shut for a nice bonus of a million dollars, and all your trouble will go away. Just go spend time with the kid, and everything is good, okay?"

Ron Ron's stress level went down immediately. "Thanks, J.R, you know I'm not used to shit like that. I love my wife. I guess I got caught up in the hype, all the money, and—"

J.R cut him off. "Look, you don't have to explain, my boy. Go handle business and keep living. Everything is good." They dapped up, and the meeting was over.

Boss Power 3

A few nights later, Beezy was wrapping up a meeting with Cold Cash Records about the upcoming forty-city tour for the Corner Boyz, via flat screen conference call at the management office alongside his assistant that ran the company mostly when Beezy was out of town for J.R or having meetings with the kingpins or handling any one of his other businesses. At this point, he owned a few sports bars, a night club that was doing very well, and I can't forget his clothing line Grind Mode, which was flying off the racks in stores and online. He was spending way less time in the street. Actually, he was barely in it at this point. His lieutenant and underboss damn near handled everything, mostly upon his order though, of course; but he was getting very squeaky-clean like J.R, not touching drugs, not being seen but in legitimate places, looking very professional. J.R had rubbed off on him a lot, and as the meeting ended, he sat there after he poured a glass of scotch. He was thinking like, at this point, the Corner Boyz and his girl group that was climbing the charts along with his other legit income could really be enough for him to leave the street. And let's not forget that Porsha's money was way up as well, but he also thought at that very moment how he was addicted to the lifestyle J.R and Umbrella was providing for him, which was unmatched. And he would have to downgrade a lot.

Porsha texted him and said, "Call when you can."

He called immediately. "Hey, wassup, bae. Everything okay?"

"Hey, yes. I just wanted to let you know I just got back to Virginia. I'm at the airport in Richmond. I think I will just sleep at our apartment this way. I have a lot of paperwork to do, and I really don't feel like driving." For a second, Beezy thought the worst, thinking that J.R was in Richmond. But that thought faded as soon as he remembered that J.R had flown to Los Angeles that morning.

He said, "Cool, let's have breakfast together in the morning or better yet lunch."

She said, "Okay, bae, I miss you." After they said their goodbyes and I love yous, he realized he was super hungry. He been handing business all day and barely ate. He texted his underboss, Li'l Ray, who used to be his underboss when he was kingpin in Norfolk. He brought him along with him when his position upgraded. Sure, Li'l Ray could have gone up to lieutenant in Norfolk, but Beezy trusted him more with his new life than anybody else. He told Li'l Ray to have the driver pull up in fifteen minutes. He wanted to go to his sports bar he owned called LB's. It was a fast-growing spot, and the wings were delicious. He wanted some, so that's what he did. When he arrived, the manager approached him, thinking something was wrong. He said, "Mr. Powell, is everything okay? I didn't know you were coming tonight."

Beezy smiled and said, "No, Thomas, I'm only coming to get some wings, no business tonight. Could you have someone bring me a six piece fried hard and a glass of scotch?"

The manager said, "Yes, Mr. Powell, it will be ready for you in a second."

"Thanks, Thomas." Beezy then got comfortable, looking through his phone and checking emails as a group of women walked in and sat at the bar. They all were pretty, but one caught his attention immediately. She was light skinned, around five feet three, had wavy hair, a sexy walk, a slim build but was curvy. They all grabbed menus, looking through them, when the bartender asked if they wanted anything to drink. They replied with each one of their choices. After the drinks were made, the bartender then told them drinks were on the house all night courtesy of Mr. Powell, which was Beezy, and pointed him out sitting at his table. He also let them know he was the owner.

He was, in fact, LB, and the name of the spot was LB's. They all smiled and sent their thank-yous. After about a half hour, one of the servers tapped the pretty chick Beezy had his eyes on when they first walked in and asked her, "Would you join Mr. Powell at his table?"

She looked over, feeling really buzzed, and said, "Sure, why not?"

When she sat down, he shook her hand and said, "I'm Brandon Powell, but my friends call me Beezy or LB. What would your name be?"

She smiled and said, "My name is Tawsia Farrell."

Beezy then said, "It's nice to meet you."

She replied, "Likewise."

He then said, "I appreciate you coming to sit with me, being that I'm a stranger."

Then she said, "After how nice you have been to me and my friends with our two-hundred-dollar tab, coming to speak is the least I could do."

He smiled and said, "Oh no, that's nothing. Hopefully, I could get to know you a li'l bit if you don't mind."

She asked and said, "So what do you want to know?"

He replied, "Anything, I just want to see your pretty lips move."

She blushed so hard that she got a little red. Between her buzz and his compliments, she was really feeling herself. They went on with a lot of flirting and small talk up until her friends were ready to go. Beezy told them, "I could never let you pretty ladies drive under the influence like that." He texted his underboss and told him to have the driver take some of his guests at the sports bar anywhere they wanted to go. Once the car came, he was about to ask Tawsia for her number. Before he could, she uttered the words, "Wow, you trying to get rid of me?"

With a light laugh, Beezy then said, "Not at all. I knew your friends were ready, so I assumed you were."

She then jokingly said, "Break down the word *assume*."

Beezy said, "Ass-u-me." And he put his hand on his face, grinning. They both then laughed. He said, "Well, you can continue to hang out with me if you want. It's been a long day for me in a lot of meetings. I am just going to my nearby condo, have one last drink, and get some rest. I have a lunch meeting tomorrow." Not mentioning that it was with his girlfriend, Porsha.

She said, "What a coincidence. I have to meet with my boss tomorrow as well. You might as well invite me for that night cap."

Beezy said quickly, "Of course! Of course!" He told Li'l Ray to go enjoy the rest of his night; he would be okay. He had his lieutenant to drop his Zenvo ST1 off at the sports bar where he was at, and after he did, Beezy and Tawsia left the spot, arriving at his condo fifteen minutes later. When they got in, he gave his maid a hundred-dollar bill. Beezy always tipped her whenever he came to that spot or any other maids that would be at one of his many homes. He told her she could have the rest of the night and next morning off. She said, "Thank you," and left. Now I could sit here and tell you that they talked all night till they fell asleep, but that's not what happened.

In the middle of their drink, she then said, "Listen, we are both grown. We both had a long day, well, a long week as well. We are both getting money."

She giggled. "I can't speak for you on this, but I'm horny as shit, so fuck me and really good. Me and my ex have been apart a couple months now. I haven't had any probably a few months prior to that, while he was out sleeping around, and I'm feeling good tonight and I want it."

Beezy went into thought mode, immediately thinking about Porsha as he lusted. Tawsia was looking so good at that moment. As he was super buzzed on top-shelf scotch, he also thought about how distant he and Porsha became and how he felt that she wanted J.R on the low. Those thoughts that were the excuses in his mind he needed to go through with the long night of hardcore fucking he and Tawsia did. They were going position after position, no slow moving, all fast as she got wetter by the stroke. They were both impressed by each other, thinking this night was perfect, and it was. They both fell asleep. This was a stress reliever they both needed.

EPISODE 36

Business as Usual

The next day was like any other normal day. Beezy called J.R to see if there was any special info he needed him to know. But J.R told him, "Nah, just continue on with normal business, and he is gonna spend the next few days with his son and Yasmine." He was very persistent to give her and his son the proper amount of time spent juggling between business and Tianna. He sent her and her mom shopping in Berlin and lots of activities for a week.

Beezy then said, "Cool." They hung up, as his driver took him to Richmond to meet with Porsha. He felt kinda bad about his night with Tawsia for a minute, but then he shook it off and said, "You know what, that was one night and that was it." He and Tawsia didn't even exchange numbers, believe it or not. They just played in the moment and enjoyed it. As he arrived at Lemaire, a very expensive restaurant in Richmond, Porsha spotted the car and went and greeted him. They kissed and walked in the spot, catching up with each other because they were separated for 80 percent of the week. After lunch, they both rode back to the 757, and Porsha wanted to stop at her shop in the beach. She had to meet up with her best hairdresser with a huge amount of clientele and was requested by many and made six figures a year. She asked Beezy to tag along before he went to handle business so they could spend a little more time together. When they arrived, Beezy told his driver and Li'l Ray to give him a few in the spot to hang out with Porsha a li'l longer. The shop was packed. Lots of money was floating through, and Porsha said, "Where is she?"

Beezy said, "Who?"

She said, "My beautician. I have to meet and discuss upgrading her to a bigger shop."

Beezy said, "Oh."

At that moment Porsha said, "There she go."

Beezy was looking through his phone as the woman came in the shop, walking right up to Porsha. "Hey, girl," they both said as Beezy paid them no mind.

The beautician told Porsha, "Girl, sorry I'm late. I had a long night, went out with my girls, met this guy, and I can't lie I went home with him and had an explosive night. I ain't no hoe, but I needed that."

Beezy said to himself, *That voice sounds familiar.* He looked up, and he and the beautician then looked at each other and their eyes got super wide. It was Tawsia, and by the energy, she could tell Beezy was there with Porsha and it was not business. She then switched the conversation immediately, feeling ashamed as well. Beezy put his head down fast.

Porsha then said, "Girl, I feel you. As businesswomen, we gotta enjoy ourselves when we can, and you got yours." She was laughing, not knowing who she got it from. She then said, "Sorry for being rude, Tawsia. This is my fiancé, Brandon, but everyone calls him LB. You probably have been to his bar before, maybe."

Tawsia replied, "Ahhhh, nah, I don't think so." She and Beezy shook hands quickly, not looking at each other too much.

Beezy said, "Bae, I have to go. The guys are waiting for me." His and Tawsia's hearts were beating fast.

Tawsia was thinking, *Out of all guys, why my boss, man?*

Beezy kissed Porsha and got out of there fast. After he left, Porsha jokingly said to Tawsia, "Speaking of getting some, he better be ready for me tonight. It's been a week."

Tawsia sarcastically thought, *It damn sure ain't been a week for him.*

Riding quietly in the back of his Bentley, Beezy was searching through Instagram, looking for Tawsia Farrell. He found her and immediately hit her DM. "Wow, Why didn't you tell me you worked for Porsha?"

She replied, "Ummm, I didn't think I was supposed to tell you who my employer was, but most importantly, why did you fail to mention you had a fiancé? And why would you call me over to sit with you?"

Beezy left her message on read for a few minutes and then replied, "Look, you wouldn't understand. I have a huge workload daily. Yes, you see my lifestyle, and it looks amazing. But to live this lifestyle, I put in a lot of long hours seven days a week, controlling several different operations. It's not easy, but to make it worse, me and Porsha are not in an exact great place. I know it may not seem that way from our behavior at the shop, but there's definitely some insecurities between us and we barely see each other. I guess after my exhausting day yesterday, several glasses of scotch, and then seeing you walk in so beautiful, I guess I got stuck in the moment and then our connection sealed the deal. It was the breath of fresh air I needed after a hard day. You was there to make me smile, and I promise I didn't expect sex. But with it happening, it made a great situation even better. It was the perfect therapy I needed."

Tawsia sat for a minute then replied, "Too bad it's over now, goodbye."

Even though she said goodbye, she totally agreed with Beezy about their connection, and after reading his reply, it made her start to feel him deeply because of his sincerity. It turned her on. She originally planned to pretend like nothing ever happened and move forward, but now she kinda wanted to spend more time with him. And after minutes of deciding it, she messaged him her number with a kiss behind it. Beezy was confused at first when he saw the number, but then he smiled, realizing he would get to see her again.

As weeks went by, they were spending a lot of time together on the low. Porsha was still traveling for J.R and Ron Ron to keep the salons all over afloat and keep the sales up. Beezy bought a new car that Porsha and her family never saw, as well as a nice condo in Suffolk, knowing none of her family stayed out there. He and Tawsia were fucking damn near every day, going to nice restaurants, catching Broadway shows in New York whenever he went out there to do business or check in on the C-Boyz, which was doing much better after taking Beezy's advice. Now their money situation was better, but Beezy and Tawsia were having so much fun. It reminded him of how he and Porsha use to be. He felt bad but good at the same time, and his passion for Porsha was fading by the day, even though he still cared for her. At this point, it seemed like everybody in the crew had their own li'l dysfunctional relationship situation. J.R seemed to have his under control. Beezy was on some "I don't care at the moment" thing. This felt too great to stop. Ron Ron was good. He just didn't know what would happen if Amelia decided to tell Elmyra even though she agreed not to say anything.

EPISODE 37

Season Finale

B esides all of them juggling their women, a situation was brewing up. Revell called J.R like, "Yo, we might have a problem." J.R replied, "Wassup?"

Revell continued, "Your Suffolk kingpin passed the word to me to let Beezy know some dude that was kinda, and I say *kinda* only because it was said he wasn't exactly on your level, but it was the closest out of the city at that time. Dude that was kinda your competition just came home from the feds and set up in some of our spots with his people, but instead of me telling Beezy, I thought I would call you personally since you know this person."

J.R responded, "Yeah, I know exactly who you talkin' bout, and nah, he's nowhere near competition. But he had a little power and influence in the street. That was back when Steph got locked up and he tried to take over the hood, but I had the Steph connect so he couldn't keep up with me. My money was on another level. My hoes were badder. My cars were more expensive. My power was too strong to compete, so he went out his way to come up as much as he could until he started selling to this undercover FBI agent for about a year. They were building a case on 'em. His bread was getting bigger, but he got indicted and sent up the road. I guess he finally out. Yeah, go let that fool know he gotta talk to me if he wanna get money in the 757 or Virginia period for that matter."

Revell then said, "Say less." Not even an hour passed and a group of dudes was posted on Broad Street in Williamstown kinda deep. Two R8 Spyder Quattro Audis pulled up and had the whole block looking. All the kids and chicks started running up, looking excited. The cars parked right in front of the group of dudes. The drivers stayed in, but one dude from each car got out holding P-416s. Then Revell stepped out, looking real serious and immediately said, "Which one of y'all niggas named Man Man?"

A dude walked from out of the middle of the crowd, trying to look like a tough guy, and said, "Yo, I know who y'all are, but tell J.R if he wanna talk to me, come to the hood and sit down with me just like the old days, none of this fancy shit. I heard he was way up and rich now. I hope he not too good to come out here and chop it up with me. Is he?"

Revell was sitting there, confused as to why J.R was even wasting his time, trying to even negotiate or whatever this was with this bum. He was obviously washed up and broke, trying to come back up. Revell just wanted to take him out real quick and get this be over with, but this was J.R's orders. And he knew J.R did everything for a reason. So he told 'em, "Okay, bet. But look, tell your goons to calm their tough-guy faces down. Trust me y'all don't want this smoke." The crowd of dudes was looking pissed after that. Revell got back in the car and drove off, texting J.R, immediately saying, "He wants you to come see him. Yo, J.R, you want me to smoke this bum ass washed-up gangster?"

J.R said, "Nah, I got this. Just send word to his people that we sitting down tonight downtown."

Revell then said, "Bet, I'm on it."

Later on that night, a brand-new Rolls Royce Wraith pulled up to the same group of dudes. This time, they had their hands on their guns. The window rolled down. It was J.R. He said, "Tell Man Man to come talk to me." Seconds later, he walked up to his car. J.R said, "Get in. I came, dolo. Tell your people you'll be back." They drove off, getting straight to business. "So wassup, how did you get out so fast? It ain't been thirty years, not even half."

Man Man replied, "Look, all those charges didn't stick. I didn't get thirty years. That was just a rumor."

J.R was thinking, *That's bullshit.* So wassup, why you send your people to my block?"

J.R replied, "Your block? Look, my boy a lot of shit changed since you left. Other than the fact I'm still getting money and you still nowhere near close to me, but fuck all that. I'm in a nice mood, and you grew up in the hood just like me. So I'ma let you get a little money out there. I even know somebody that can supply you the best for the cheapest."

Man Man replied, "You mean you, right?"

J.R said, "Me? No you must be misinformed. I'm in the music business. My boy, I don't touch drugs no more." This was the truth. He didn't touch drugs, but he was definitely moving tons of it indirectly.

But anyway, Man Man said, "I heard you were running the whole 757 now."

J.R said, "Look, I do business with a lot of people, all legit. I'm getting money all kinds of ways, so you know how much muhfuckas think you gotta be selling drugs."

Man Man got quiet, looking around, and said, "So wassup? You're saying the game wide open for me then?"

J.R said, "It's all yours. As a matter of fact, I'ma even hit you with a li'l money to get you on your feet." They pulled up to a big house out in Portsmouth. When they got in the driveway, somebody came and opened J.R's door and had an umbrella waiting for him as it was now raining kinda heavy. They all went inside.

Man Man was looking around amazed and said, "This crib nice as shit."

J.R replied, "It's okay. I got better ones than this, but fuck all that. Have a drink with me. A badass Puerto Rican chick came up with a bottle of good cognac and poured them a drink. They talked and talked. J.R said, "Yeah, so will a couple million get you on your feet?"

Man Man said, "Yeah, but you sure you not the plug?"

That statement right there confirmed all of J.R's suspensions. *I mean after somebody offered you two million dollars, I think I would see more excitement than that instead of worrying if I were the plug or not.* He knew exactly what was up. J.R laughed and said, "Damn, my nigga, I never thought you would go out like a sucka."

Man Man said, "What?"

J.R said, "Look, enough of the games." He snapped his fingers, and the same chick that poured the drinks came back out, walked up to Man Man, took a razor, and sliced his shirt straight down the middle. All you saw was wire. J.R was shaking his head. She then sliced the wire in half. J.R pulled out his .44 Magnum. Man Man damn near pissed his pants and said, "J.R, no, man, they made me do it. They said if I didn't, they would kill my kids. I promise I was gonna tell you."

J.R said, "When? After I was locked up? Man, fuck all that. Let me get one thing clear. I run this state, and yeah I am the plug in Virginia and outside. Trust me, the second you showed up, I could have sent a hit and took you out instantly, but I knew better. I knew yo' hating ass was snitching. You always felt some type of way about me doing better than you, and when you found out I was on the level I was, you couldn't help yourself. You had to try and put them people on me, but I'm not your average cat. I'm always steps ahead if I would have gotten you killed. The second you showed up, the FBI would have known it was me, but guess what, that ankle bracelet you got on about to get in a car and travel for miles. So they going to think you running. As far as me, I'm in a meeting in LA according to Cold Cash Records, who just tweeted about a huge signing with my newest CA artist signed to my management company. So the voice they was hearing on that wire could have been anybody you pretended to be me to make your escape. So your li'l plan failed."

Man Man said quickly, "Come on, J.R. It's not like that."

J.R shook his head and started putting bullets back to back in Man Man's chest. Revell then walked in and said, "Damn, J.R, you couldn't wait for me?" They both laughed.

J.R said, "Nah, this was personal. I had to do it myself."

Revell then said, "Well, I see you still got it."

J.R said, "No doubt, somebody clean this shit up." He put on his jacket, grabbed the whole bottle of cognac, and got out of there.

Even though J.R carefully handled that situation, he knew right then that the feds were on his radar from this clown Man Man attempting to snitch and set him up. Even if they couldn't prove it at the moment, they damn sure started raiding a lot of his spots in the 757. Some of his higher rank was arrested. Usually a few runners and lookouts might get jammed up in the past, but now some lieutenants and a couple of underbosses' houses were kicked in and charged with drugs, murder, and etc. Ron Ron's legal team had a heavy workload at this point because this was happening back to back. Northern Virginia wasn't hot, so he sent the biggest amount of drugs up that way, shutting down certain spots in Hampton Roads until things cooled down, as well as doubled up on out-of-town clientele to make up for what he couldn't move at home. Either way, he had to get the plug his money, so the show had to continue no matter what. J.R was back in shark mode. Anybody that even seemed to be suspicious was killed immediately. He didn't trust nothing or nobody at this point. He was prepared to get police hit if necessary.

After weeks of being extra cautious, J.R was exhausted. He barely got any sleep, traveling more than usual, and being very hands-on lately with the operation. He didn't know who to trust outside of his immediate team. His birthday was coming up, and he just wanted to spend time with his son and see Yasmine. He hadn't been to California the past couple weeks, and he planned to do so. But first he took Tianna on a very expensive shopping spree. They wined and dined and made love over and over. Tianna really enjoyed spending time with J.R, especially because usually he was on the go. She knew his birthday was coming up, and she knew he was going to LA to do some business with Billy. Well at least that was what he told her, but anyway, she planned to surprise him. She already booked her hotel and her first-class plane ticket. Now usually J.R would never let Tianna or Yasmine fly on a commercial flight. It was private jets only, but Tianna had no access to one. And this was a surprise, so the flight was necessary. She knew J.R usually dined at his favorite sports bar, one of many he opened out there. He took her there a few times before. When that time came, she pretended she and her sisters were going on a cruise. J.R left that morning after making love to Tianna and having a great breakfast in bed. He left his black card for her in the living room and had his driver pick him up, heading to his jet. When he landed, he texted Yasmine and let her know he would see her later. That night, he did handle a little business, as well as had a meeting with a new potential client to supply a large amount. Just as Tianna suspected, he went to his favorite spot out there. He wanted to sip cognac and clear his mind for a moment before going home to Yasmine and getting his birthday started. Tianna's whole plan was working perfectly. She had the best lingerie Myla had to offer. She took a long nice bath then put on J.R's favorite fragrance, as well as lingerie and coat.

She drove up to the bar J.R was at, waiting patiently in the parking lot. She planned to follow his car to his hotel and then knock at his door to surprise him. She was excited. When J.R felt he had one drink too many, he texted his driver to pull up. J.R got in the back seat as Tianna started up her rental car and followed the Rolls Royce J.R was riding in. The drive was maybe thirty minutes, pulling up to this beautiful estate. Not a hotel as Tianna thought. For a second, she thought maybe he was going to handle more business, but when she saw J.R get out and unlock the door with a key, she then said, "Wow, maybe this house is a surprise for me." So after she parked, she saw the time was close to twelve, and she just wanted to hug and kiss him and tell him happy birthday and make his day, as well as blow his mind all night.

J.R went inside and went immediately to the shower to freshen up. With the shower running, he didn't hear the doorbell. On the other side of the door as Tianna stood there, the door opened, but to her surprise, it wasn't J.R. It was a beautiful mixed black and Asian woman holding a baby. Of course, it was Yasmine, and she was smiling, knowing exactly who Tianna was. And Tianna was standing there, looking confused and wondering who this chick and baby were.

Yasmine said, "Can I help you?"

Tianna replied, "Yes, I think my fiancé lives here. His name is J.R."

Yasmine then said, "Do you mean my son's father, J.R?"

Everything went quiet for Tianna. Her heart was beating extremely fast. She was so hurt at that moment. She forced herself

inside, running through the huge house, looking for J.R, and scream-
ing his name. But he didn't hear because of the shower. As she checked
every room, she finally went into one of the upstairs bathrooms he
was in. He turned and saw Tianna, and his heart dropped. He didn't
know what to say as he saw tears going down Tianna's face, saying, "I
knew it was too good to be true." She ran out of the bathroom then
out of the house, being chased by J.R, who was soaking wet with a
towel wrapped around him. Tianna got to her car and drove off fast
while Yasmine sat there, hurt as well, realizing J.R was probably more
in love with Tianna than her.

J.R was panicking, thinking he was probably gonna lose Tianna,
and that thought felt like a sharp knife. He couldn't even regroup and
get himself together before he got a call from his sport's bar manager
that the bar was just raided and the warrant was for J.R. He was
like, "Huh?" Before he could ask why, his other line was Stacey. He
clicked over, and she quickly said, "J.R, where are you? Don't panic,
but shit is a little fucked up. Beezy and Revell were arrested by the
FBI, and they sent a team to California to grab you before you could
even be warned. My advice as your attorney is to just turn yourself
in, and I will handle everything. Please don't run. It will only make
things harder for me to get you out of this."

J.R said, "But what the fuck did I do? What's going on?"

Stacey, with an excited voice, said, "The charge is murder and
accessory to murder. Apparently, Revell shot Steve Wilson down in
downtown Portsmouth not too long ago There were no initial wit-
nesses who would talk because everyone knew who Revell was and
who he is associated with, which is you. Across the street at the gas
station was a camera that the feds reviewed with permission of the
owner, which is from another country, not knowing you or your
power. On the camera for that day, it showed Revell gunning Steve
down in broad daylight, as well as spotting Beezy there at the scene
of the crime. But the license plate was registered to you, J.R Jones, so
they think you sent the hit."

J.R then screamed, "SHIT!" He did not know what to do. Was
Tianna going to leave him? Were the feds about to lock him up? He
called and called Tianna for the next couple of hours. There was no

answer. He took Stacey's advice and turned himself in. It only made it easier for her to defend him and to make a bad situation worse. Billy texted him, saying, "Shit about to be dry for a few. The connect had to slow down for a few due to him being investigated." So that was Tianna gone. He was facing a murder charge, and his plug was falling back for a while. Everything was happening all at once. He was booked that same night with no contact with Beezy or Revell. They were booked in Virginia where J.R would be extradited in the morning. He couldn't get Tianna off his brain, and he was thinking, *How would this operation go on if the supply is about to stop for a while?*

Well, the only way to know what happens next is tune in to the next season of *Street Wealthy*.

About the Author

L arry Darnell Darden Jr. was born in Suffolk, Virginia, on July 20, 1981. He started writing at the age of eight but in the form of music. At eleven years old was when he became serious about the craft of writing music. He evolved to writing books because his imagination was full of ideas that he needed to express. A coworker and friend helped inspire him as they often joked together about a fictional character. His upbringing and experiences led him to develop fictional character and create many more. His intelligence played a factor in creating a book. He enjoys writing books and have many more to come.